23 MINUTES

VIVIAN VANDE VELDE

BOYDS MILLS PRESS
AN IMPRINT OF HIGHLIGHTS
Honesdale, Pennsylvania

Boyds Mills Press
An Imprint of Highlights
815 Church Street
Honesdale, Pennsylvania 18431

Printed in the United States of America
ISBN: 978-1-62979-441-9 (hc)
ISBN: 978-1-62979-561-4 (e-book)

Library of Congress Control Number: 2015953497

First edition
The text of this book is set in Chaparral.
Design by Barbara Grzeslo
Production by Sue Cole
10 9 8 7 6 5 4 3 2 1

Dedicated to those
who try to make things better
for at-risk children and teens

CHAPTER 1

THE STORY STARTS WITH AN ACT OF STUNNING VIOLENCE.

Or . . . well . . . maybe not exactly.

Maybe, exactly, the story starts when Zoe walks into the bank—except she doesn't recognize it as a story yet. She just knows the sky has opened up in a late-autumn downpour so that she feels as though she's standing under the shower at the campground— the one that's strong and steady but has only two temperatures: cold and very cold. Zoe has never understood the point of camping. Haven't people evolved for thousands of years precisely so that they do *not* have to sleep on the ground, or pee and crap outdoors, or have to eat half-raw food that's been charred over a fire? But the people who run group homes for teens nobody wants to foster always seem to feel that "roughing it" is a way to Build Community Spirit. And to Bond with the Disadvantaged Youth of Our City. As though they weren't in a group home exactly because they'd had a rough time already. Zoe feels that an overnight at a Holiday Inn, hanging out in the hot tub, ordering room service, and watching on-demand movies, would make much more satisfying building and bonding experiences. Not that anybody has ever asked Zoe.

So the rain starts fast and hard and just a degree or two warmer than sleet, and Zoe dashes through the first door she comes to and finds herself in a bank.

That's more a prelude than a beginning to the story: the foreword, the setup.

Then there are the supporting characters: the snotty bank teller and the full-of-himself bank guard. As well as the one bank customer, the one who stands out from the fewer-than-a-dozen other customers—the young guy Zoe immediately pegs as an up-and-coming business exec or a junior lawyer at a prestigious law firm (the kind that does *not* advertise on TV). Zoe prides herself on being able to evaluate people quickly. It's been a necessity for survival. But this guy has an engaging smile and takes the time to speak kindly to her, even after she walks into him, steps on his foot, and drips rainwater on him and his expensive shoes. Lastly, and of course, there's the bank robber—although Zoe doesn't know yet that he *is* a bank robber.

Not much here to say *story*.

It doesn't really pick up speed until the robbery starts to go awry, until they're all within twenty feet of each other—even closer if you're willing to discount that one bank teller. Without her, they're really in a tight cluster: Zoe on her knees on the floor, the guard with his gun drawn and aimed at the head of the would-be robber, the would-be robber with *his* gun drawn and aimed at the head of the guy who was nice to Zoe.

Should I say it now? she wonders, several times, until finally, after all the shouting and gun-waving and threatening to shoot anyone and everyone, the robber's attention is firmly on someone else besides Zoe. *Finally*, she sees she might actually have a moment or two in which to use her special ability and get away.

If only that opportunity weren't a result of the young CEO (or whatever he is) intentionally stepping between her and the robber.

Is he stupid or suicidal? Zoe asks herself.

But this is unfairly diminishing him. His eyes are blue and wide and have enough fear in them to say he knows exactly what he's done, enough defiance to declare he'd make the same choice again.

And that holds Zoe where she is.

The situation gets even worse, with more shouting, more threatening—and then there are two simultaneous shots. Or too close to simultaneous to make a difference.

Leaving Zoe spattered in the blood of both the thief and the customer she'd almost had time to grow to like. Not to mention bits of bone. And what she very fervently tries to convince herself could not possibly really be pieces of brain matter.

That's how the story starts.

CHAPTER 2

OK . . . PERHAPS THAT'S A BIT TOO SPARE A TELLING.

So, for this one time only: a playback of the exact same twenty-three minutes, just with more detail.

Which, of course, is totally *not* the way Zoe's ability to play back time works. Not that Zoe understands much about how it *does* work.

Sometimes she speculates that she was born this way and just didn't discover it until she became a teen, that it's a latent, half-baked magical capability, or some sort of genetic mutation inflicted on her by a universe with a twisted sense of humor. She likes the idea that there might, in fact, be others like her—even if, by playback's very nature, that would be hard, if not impossible, to know.

Or maybe the skill or knack or talent came because she almost died at age ten, when her appendix burst, after her mother waited so long to bring her to the doctor because—as Mom explained at the hospital—"She's always complaining about something."

Or it may all have started that time Zoe was twelve, when she remained outside during a storm, watching nature's show, the smell of ozone tickling her nose. She could feel the hairs on her arms stand up as the rumbles of thunder came just about simultaneous to the jags of lightning—closer and closer, and louder and brighter, till that one bolt of lightning hit the flagpole in the Durans' yard right next door, throwing Zoe off the steps and onto her back, her whole body a-tingle with electrical spiders. At twelve, Zoe knew enough not to seek solace from her mother for what had just happened, knew how her mother would have reacted: by giving Zoe a taste of the back of her hand, chiding, "Stupid thing—without the sense to come in out of the rain. You got what you deserved."

However . . . whenever . . . whyever the ability to play back time came to her, Zoe has it, and has been aware of having it for two and a half years now, since she was thirteen.

Zoe is walking in the downtown shopping area, not shopping, but with nowhere to go, when the clouds suddenly burst with Noah-and-the-ark ferocity. She shoves her folder of papers under her t-shirt, but the rain is cold and relentless, so she ducks into the nearest doorway, which is a branch of Spencerport Savings and Loan. This is not an especially good choice, as there is not much for a fifteen-year-old who doesn't even have a bank account to do here. Zoe rubs her arms—one at a time because she still has the folder pressed protectively against herself—and wishes she'd brought her jacket when she left this morning.

No, what Zoe really wishes is that she could play back the entire day. A do-over starting with not mouthing off to Mrs. Davies.

But twenty-three minutes is her limit, and twenty-three minutes after her confrontation with Mrs. Davies, Zoe was still too angry to even *think* about backing off. Now it's way too late to do anything about it.

Too damn impulsive—she's heard *that* before.

Besides, she knows from past experience what a slippery thing playing back time can be. She has used it in instances both serious and frivolous, and she estimates she has a ten percent chance of actually improving any given initial situation. Her mind goes—as it so often does lately when she thinks about playback—to how she progressed from tongue-tied to awkwardly flirting to successfully flirting with that cute guy at the bus stop . . . only to find out that the guy was her best friend Delia's new love interest, who was supposed to be waiting for Delia. And no minutes left to play back to ignoring him. Delia still hasn't forgiven her—and that's without knowing anything about playback, so she doesn't even have a clue how relentlessly Zoe pursued him.

In the two and a half years she's had this ability, playback has cost her more than it's gained, and Zoe has come to think of her life as being like one of those choose-your-own-adventure books—one where it's best to read through once and settle, because the choices only go from bad to worse.

So, Zoe is cold and she's wet, and Mrs. Davies is pissed off at her: OK, well, there's nothing new in that.

There are about a dozen customers in the bank this afternoon, the first Friday of November. The bank guard standing inside, just by the entrance, is looking at her with suspicion and disapproval, perhaps for dripping puddles onto the floor, perhaps because he suspects she has chosen the bank as a place for hanging around with her teenage hoodlum friends, now that the mall three blocks over has instituted a policy prohibiting teens from being there unless they're accompanied by a parent.

His level of concern is not appeased even after she pulls her folder from under her shirt and goes to the tall table that has cubbyholes for deposit and withdrawal slips. Whereas the folder itself is water-spotted, the papers inside are undamaged. That's good. She supposes. Although, now that she's calmed down after her skirmish with Mrs. Davies, she has to ask herself: How important, really, are these papers? Probably not worth the trouble she's in.

Zoe takes a pink bank slip, without even looking close enough to see whether it's for deposits or withdrawals. She picks up the pen, which—for all that it looks like the kind sold by the dozen at the dollar store—is attached to the counter by a chain. Then she turns the bank slip over, and on the empty back side writes down the names of the other girls on her floor. There is no particular reason for doing this other than to see if she can remember them all, and mostly to take up time. She starts with Delia, even though Delia is no longer speaking to her.

Another slip of paper, and she works on recording the names of all the actors who have played James Bond in the movies. Yet another slip for Snow White's seven dwarves. And another for Santa's reindeer. Except she can only think of eight reindeer, and if you include Rudolph—which she has—she knows there should be nine.

All right, she can't stay at this table all afternoon. Although she refuses to glance in his direction, because that would make her look as though she has a guilty conscience, she's sure the guard is watching her and counting the number of slips she's using up.

Zoe stuffs the slips into her folder and gets in line to wait for the next available teller, hoping this will indicate to the guard that she has legitimate bank business.

That next available teller turns out to sound as disapproving as the guard looks when she asks Zoe, "May I help you?" As though she resents having to pretend someone like Zoe is a genuine customer.

As though she suspects Zoe is here to ask for a handout, or to try to sell candy to support her school's soccer team, despite the sign by the door that says "No Soliciting"—which, in this neighborhood, could mean candy or something else entirely. Zoe speaks right up, knowing instinctively that this teller is the kind of adult who feels that all kids mumble. She asks, "Do you have any of those presidential dollars?"

The woman's smile does not seem any less forced than her offer to be of assistance. "Who are you looking for?"

Zoe does not tell her that, grammatically speaking, this should be: *For whom are you looking?* In a world of shifting group homes and social workers who burn out or move on just when you get used to them, Zoe likes the order imposed on language by grammar. Still, she generally tries to avoid attention. So she simply answers, "William Henry Harrison."

William Henry Harrison is Zoe's favorite president. He was only in office for thirty-two days, and he was sick for just about all of them, since he caught pneumonia at his inauguration, and then he died. Zoe figures you just have to love someone who's that damn unlucky.

"Harrison . . ." The teller opens her change drawer and looks through some loose coins, murmuring, "Pierce . . . Adams . . . other Adams . . . FDR . . . ," perhaps thinking Zoe might be convinced to revise her presidential dollar needs. "No, sorry." Yet another insincere smile.

"That's OK," Zoe says. She isn't even sure, now that she thinks about it, whether she has a dollar's worth of change in her pocket to pay for a presidential dollar.

12

She steps away from the teller counter. There's a coffee bar set up on a low table in the sitting area, with a sign that says "COMPLIMENTARY COFFEE FOR OUR CUSTOMERS." Outdoors, it's still pouring, and coffee would certainly help chase away the chill in her bones, but she wonders if asking for and not receiving a William Henry Harrison dollar qualifies her as a customer.

Without glancing at the guard to see if he's still watching her, she goes back to the bank-slips stand, which is just to the side of the row of tellers. She opens her folder. She shuffles her papers. Takes yet another slip from its cubbyhole and once again tries for the reindeer names. Still only eight. She compares with her previous list, hoping it's a different eight; but, no, there's someone she's consistently leaving out.

And still no sign of the rain letting up. Zoe decides she will take the drenching required to cross the street to the card shop. She might even find something appropriate for Mrs. Davies. It would be just like Hallmark to have a line of cards for people who need to apologize to their housemothers. Not that Zoe would actually *buy* a card. But she could memorize a suitable sentiment.

Just as she steps away from the table, into the bank strides a twitchy, self-absorbed-looking man who obviously takes the weather as a personal affront. Zoe can tell all this from his posture, since he's huddled into his raincoat: head down, shoulders up, hands jammed into pockets. He nearly plows into Zoe, proving yet again what Zoe already knows: Kids, even older kids who have done their best to make themselves look tough, are invisible.

Zoe takes a hurried step back despite her oft-declared opinion that the world would be a better place if people would simply refrain from walking in any direction they aren't actually facing.

And so she walks backward onto the foot of the young man, a customer who has come to use the deposit or withdrawal slips.

"Oh, I'm sorry," he says—polite, not sarcastic—even though *she* and not *he* is the one clearly at fault. He catches hold of her left elbow—possibly to keep her from falling, since she's off-balance; possibly simply to protect himself from further trampling.

The forms Zoe has been pretending to fill out slide free from her folder and flutter floor-ward, along with a few of the pages she has risked Mrs. Davies's wrath to get hold of.

"I am such an idiot," Zoe mutters.

"No, really, this sort of thing happens to everyone."

The young man has paperwork of his own, though he has sensibly chosen to keep his held securely in one of those pouch-like office envelopes that close with a string. Still, he crouches down to help retrieve Zoe's papers. He's probably only eight or nine years older than she is, but at this time in their lives that's a pretty big difference: He moves with the self-assurance of an adult. A successful adult, she decides, with a snap judgment of his haircut and his clothes. Clearly, he goes to a stylist, not a simple barber or a trainee at the Rochester School of Beauty, where Zoe goes—*when* Zoe goes. And he wears his tailored jacket and button-down shirt without a tie and paired with jeans, a look she labels a bit too self-consciously trendy. She understands that her look—a ponytail coupled with thrift-shop jeans and tee—labels her a loser. Her hair is dyed blue (intentionally so) and is cut raggedly (more happenstance than statement). Normally, Zoe is pleased with her look, as it lets her fit in where she wants to, and pretty much scares everyone else away.

Zoe isn't familiar enough with banks to know if it's reasonable to have five separate slips (three pink and two white), but suspects it probably is not. "It's OK, it's OK," she tells the guy, snatching the papers from his hands so he can't see that she's only written on the backs of them, and that what she's written are lists of names rather than numbers, which might at least *seem* to be bank- or money-related.

"Thank you," she says. She's so intent on retrieving the bank slips that she loses track of holding tight to her folder. The rest of her papers slide free and cascade to the floor between them.

"You're welcome." His voice is nice without sounding put on. Except he's looking at one of the slips that has landed list-side-up, clearly revealing her lack of banking seriousness:

Rudolph	Vixen
Dasher	Comet
Dancer	Cupid
Donner	Prancer

He's frowning, and she's sure he's about to report her to the proper authorities. Or at the very least, to take back what he said about her not being an idiot.

But what he says is, "Blitzen." He looks up at her, and she realizes he's somewhere between friendly and amused. "The one you've left out is Blitzen."

"Thank you," Zoe repeats, aware that now she *is* mumbling.

Wonderful. He thinks she's cute in a clumsy, gawky-little-kid way. People always seem to assume short girls are younger than they really are.

As for him . . . he has good hair—light brown and well-styled—

but his features are more *interesting* than *attractive*, Zoe thinks.

However, she gives his smile an A+.

Too bad he's laughing at her.

Should she say it? she wonders, should she say *playback*—the word that will stop the orderly progression of time and rewind to twenty-three minutes earlier, to *before* she made an idiot of herself in front of this guy? *No*, she tells herself. *Duh! He's in his mid-twenties!* Since when has she been in the habit of looking appraisingly at adult men who aren't singers or actors? And besides, that would mean reliving the whole getting-caught-in-the-rain thing.

A foot comes down on the reindeer paper, and it belongs to the bank guard. And the guard asks, "Any trouble here?"

"Not at all," the young guy says, "except for . . . ,"—he indicates the paper under the guard's shoe—"the fact that you appear to be stepping on one of our papers."

Ooh, *our*. He's aligning himself with her: the two of them vs. the guard.

The guard, who has observed them come in separately, who sees how totally different from one another they are on the socially acceptable scale, seems to suspect they must be up to something, but he clearly hasn't determined *what* yet.

Almost reluctantly, the guard lifts his foot, then leans down for a closer look. Zoe shifts forward to intercept the paper before he can read it, and they clunk heads. While she and the guard are distracted, her co-conspirator with the nice jacket and the nicer smile whisks the bank slip off the floor. He wipes it on his jeans, which might be to brush off the guard's footprint, or might be an excuse to hand the paper to Zoe writing-side down.

"Thank you," she says—mumbles—again. She hurriedly jams all

16

the papers, bank slips and group home forms, back into the folder.

Jacket Guy is definitely amused, and the guard is definitely not.

Jacket stands, a quick, graceful movement, and extends a hand for Zoe, who is neither quick nor graceful despite—or maybe precisely because of—his help.

"Thank you," Jacket says to the guard. He sounds like a perfect example of impeccable manners—but he's also clearly saying, *You can go now.*

Not that she needed Jacket's help. Or anyone's. Zoe prides herself on being self-sufficient.

Rain or no rain, she determines to dash across the street to the card shop, where she won't stick out so badly; and it is at that exact moment she loses the attention of the interesting-rather-than-good-looking Jacket. He is staring beyond her with an expression she can't quite make out before his face shuts down entirely, blank and intentionally unreadable. At that same moment there's a ruckus behind her. One of the bank tellers squeals. The guard turns to see if there's something wrong going on in his bank—something more wrong than Zoe—and she sees that his hand actually starts moving toward the gun he wears on his hip, but then he freezes.

This has nothing to do with you, Zoe tells herself. *None of your business. Get out of here now.* At this moment, there seem to be several options for getting out, and playing back time is only one of them.

But if there's something dangerous going on behind her, surely she'd be better off knowing what that danger is.

Though perhaps not . . .

Because once she, too, has slowly turned around, she sees the twitchy customer, the one who entered the bank so quickly he'd almost run her down. And he has a gun. He just hasn't decided yet where to point it. He's waving it at the row of five tellers, at the customers, at the guard, who—though he has a weapon of his own—holds both hands up and away from his body in a conciliatory gesture.

It's cold out, and wet, so she had noticed without really noting that this . . . well, as it turns out, *bank robber* . . . had come in with his shoulders hunched and his raincoat collar up around his face. Now she finally takes in that he has the brim of his baseball cap pulled down, obscuring all of his hair and much of his face. And now he is standing not three feet away from Zoe.

"Hands up!" he yells, sounding for all the world like he's channeling every crazed bank thief Zoe has ever seen on TV or in the movies. "Everybody, hands up!"

Everyone obeys, even the customers who are diving behind the few pieces of furniture in this suddenly way-too-open room. Even Zoe, who lets her folder—with all its papers—slip from her arms and drop to the floor.

Which is OK, because to make the playback work, she needs to put her arms around herself. Once the thief is distracted enough not to notice her, of course.

"Hands away from the gun!" he yells at the guard, although the guard's hands are already well away from the gun.

"They are, they are!" the guard assures him.

"You!" the gunman orders the teller whose window he's at, the one who helped—or rather didn't help—Zoe. "Keep filling the bag!"

She has a canvas bag into which she's been dumping all the money from her drawer. When she finishes, clumsy because of her shaking, she looks to the gunman for further instructions. He indicates for her to hand the bag to the next teller.

"Nobody try anything!" Gun Man warns tellers and customers alike.

Although Zoe is the one who, by the unhappiest coincidence, happens to be standing closest to the thief, he's looking beyond her, watching the guard. Zoe brings her arms down and wraps them tight around herself, the first move to getting rid of this version of time. But the motion draws Gun Man's attention. He grabs hold of her arm roughly enough that the thought—the damn stupid thought—crosses her mind: *Ooh, that'll leave bruises.*

More importantly, it will also prevent the playback from working.

"Take his gun," the robber demands.

"What?" Zoe's brain is numb with the awfulness of the situation she's found herself in.

Which is no reason for him to use his free hand to slap her, the way people in movies always calm down the hysterical. Zoe has no idea why Hollywood writers seem to think a slap should have a calming influence. With her cheek red and stinging, she is more terrified than ever.

"There's no cause for that," a level voice protests, and Zoe realizes it's Jacket, who was kind to her just moments before as he tried to deflect the ire of the bank guard, now trying to deflect the robber. "She's just a kid. I'll get the gun."

In fact, he's already partway turned toward the guard, but Gun Man orders him, "Turn back around. Face me."

Don't draw attention to yourself, Zoe mentally wishes at Jacket.

Zoe has grown good at not drawing attention to herself.

Except, of course, that she's standing within being-slapped distance of a very nervous guy with a gun.

"Take the guard's gun," the robber tells Zoe. "Now. With your left hand. Two fingers only. Slowly."

Zoe hopes everyone can see she is not doing this of her own free will, that she is not part of this man's bank-robbing gang.

"Sorry," she tells the guard.

But even as she reaches for the guard's weapon, Gun Man seems to snap. He suddenly starts shooting.

People scream and cover their heads with their hands.

Zoe has seen gunshot victims before. She knows what woefully inadequate protection hands are.

But for the moment, Gun Man is only shooting at the bank's cameras. Which Zoe supposes makes sense.

It is also the point at which she realizes, *He's going to kill us all.*

Gun Man is furious about something. Zoe can't tell if it's because she's been too slow, or if someone else here has done something to tick him off, or if he's passed some mental landmark that was holding him in check, or what. He doesn't even seem to be concerned anymore about Zoe getting the guard's gun. Instead, he's fixated on the young guy in the good clothes.

What have you done? Zoe wonders at Jacket.

Besides the obvious: He's taken one big step forward. And this means he, not Zoe, is now the one standing closest to Gun Man. He still has his hands in the air, but apparently that isn't good enough.

Gun Man grabs him by his well-cut jacket and shoves him against the half-wall that separates the tellers from the rest of the bank. He has his left arm pressed against the young man's throat, and his gun pressed against his temple. "Drop the gun," he shouts at the guard. "Drop the gun or I blow this asshole's brains out."

Zoe hadn't even been aware of the guard drawing his weapon.

And of all the stupid things he could say, Jacket tells the guard, "Don't."

"You think I'm bluffing?" Gun Man demands. "I can do it. You gotta know nothing would make me happier than to do it." He twists the gun back and forth as though trying to screw it into Jacket's head.

In any case, the guard does not put down his gun. He steps right next to Zoe, and he has his gun aimed at Gun Man's head. Zoe sees the guard's hand is shaking, and surely that's not a good sign.

The tellers—very sensibly, in Zoe's estimation—all duck behind their counters.

Stop this, Zoe tells herself. *Stop it now.* She can. To a certain extent.

But she has not had good luck with this sort of thing in the past. She spent way too long on it at thirteen—she thinks she may have spent *years* playing back various moments when she was thirteen, trying to fix things, despite the fact that, really, nobody can fix being thirteen. And just a few weeks ago, there was the whole business with Delia's boyfriend, when she didn't understand the situation. Not that *this* situation seems open to a lot of interpretation.

"Take the money," Gun Man is ordering Jacket, since the bag has made its way back to the teller nearest them and is sitting right there next to him. "These nice people are going to let us walk out of here so I don't have to shoot you."

"Screw you," Jacket says. Which strikes Zoe as yet another very

21

obviously not smart thing to say.

"It's this simple," Gun Man says. "Cooperate—hope everyone cooperates—and you live. I'll release you outside."

"No, you won't," Jacket argues. He repeats the thought to the guard, as though to make sure the guard understands. "He's never going to let me go. He's never going to let any of us go. There are too many people who could identify him. So you might as well just shoot him now."

First no video witness, then no people witnesses. This is the same conclusion Zoe reached when the man shot out the cameras. Still, she can't help clutching at hope. *You don't know for a fact that he's going to kill you*, she thinks at Jacket. *Better the chance of maybe being killed later than definitely being killed now.*

Which is when she has the thought: *Is he stupid or suicidal?*

Jacket refuses to take the bag that the one teller is trying to hand him, reaching up from behind her hiding place.

The guard seems to decide that Zoe, standing so close, is in the way, and he shoves her; but she trips over her own feet and instead of ending up farther away, ends up on her knees on the floor.

Jacket is looking directly at Gun Man and tells the guard, "Take the shot."

"Even if," Gun Man hastily points out, "this clown cop could get a shot off before I could, even if he puts the bullet in my brain and I'm dead in an instant, in that instant my finger *will* tighten on the trigger, and you're dead."

"I'm dead in any case," Jacket tells the guard, and Zoe wishes he wouldn't be so sure of that. "Or he'd prove his good intentions by putting his gun down now."

Gun Man proves his bad intentions by not moving.

Jacket repeats to the guard, "Take the shot."

The guard isn't the only one whose hand is shaking. Gun Man sees his options dwindling as Jacket refuses to cooperate, and Zoe knows this makes him even more dangerous.

Say it, Zoe tells herself. *Say it now.*

She needs to risk drawing attention. She crosses her arms, hugging herself. All she needs to do is to say, "Playback," which will make all of this go away.

She falters when she sees Jacket brace himself. For what? Does he have a plan? Does he expect the gunman will see the hopelessness of getting away and back down, or does Jacket think he can overpower him? Will he dodge or duck or drop to his knees in the hope of avoiding Gun Man's bullet while giving the guard a clear shot? Or is he preparing himself to die? She's looking directly into his blue eyes and can't begin to guess what's going on behind them as he says, "Take the damn shot."

And the guard does.

Whether conscious revenge or muscle reflex, the bank robber squeezes his trigger, too.

And whatever Jacket's plan was—unless it was to die—it doesn't work.

Which brings everything back to the beginning, leaving Zoe spattered in the blood of both the thief and the customer she'd almost had time to grow to like. Not to mention bits of bone. And what she very fervently tries to convince herself could not possibly really be pieces of brain matter.

That's how the story starts.

CHAPTER 3

SOME OF THE BANK CUSTOMERS—BOTH THOSE WHO FROZE into please-please-please-don't-notice-me statues and those who dove behind chairs and tables—now take the opportunity to make a break for the door. Zoe is vaguely aware of the thudding of their feet, like antelope spooked by a lion.

Which she recognizes as being an unreasonable there-you-go-thinking-you're-better-than-they-are judgment, considering she is among the frozen. She thinks of those *National Geographic* films where you watch the stupid baby antelope, the one without the sense to even try to run, get taken down and devoured.

Still—burst appendix and thunderstorms notwithstanding—this is as close as she's ever come to dying in her fifteen years. At least, as far as she knows. She supposes the world is full of idiot drivers—really-too-old-to-be-driving or really-too-young-to-be-driving or really-too-stupid-to-be-driving drivers—who end up hitting a street sign before they have a chance to head off into oncoming traffic, so all the people who *might* have been plowed into never even know how close a call they've had. Not to mention assorted meteor strikes and flash floods and earthquakes and plagues and spontaneous combustions that might have occurred, but didn't.

But Zoe recognizes that she's intentionally trying to distract herself with some pretty lame nitpicking. The fact is, she could very easily have been killed just now—and for the moment she is still feeling more scared by the *might-have-beens* than grateful for the big *wasn't*.

One of the bank tellers is screaming—a reaction for which Zoe has no patience, not after the fact—and at least one of the customers is crying, which Zoe is more willing to accept, as she herself might give in to crying later on. It's just there's no time *now*. Not because the police are coming in, which they are, too late, carrying enough gear to attack a terrorist stronghold. But because a decision must be made. By Zoe. She must make a decision, and she doesn't want to because she knows how easily things could have gone another way, how easily the bank robber could have turned his gun on all of them.

This has nothing to do with you, Zoe reminds herself. Not for the first time since she walked into this bank. Not for the first time in her life.

She intentionally tries to avoid thinking of the young man who may well have died in her place.

She is staring so intently at her knees to avoid looking at the two dead bodies, which she's almost close enough to touch, that she does not at first see the feet and legs of the policeman who steps between her and the bodies, specifically trying to block them from her view. As though the image isn't fixed in her brain indelibly.

Despite the way she knows she looks—like a street kid, or at least a troublesome kid, neither of which she is, but that's what she looks like—despite that, the situation is such that the policeman doesn't focus on this. He puts his hand, his free hand, not the one holding the assault rifle, on her shoulder. "It's all right," he encourages her. "It's all over."

Shows how much *he* knows.

Zoe looks up the length of his black-clad legs, his flak jacket, past his face, hoping to catch sight of a clock, but she can't get beyond the blood on the wall behind him. A normal teenager would have a cell phone to tell the time, but the group home kids are not allowed to carry them.

How many minutes have passed, have been wasted by her feeling sorry for herself? Twenty-three minutes are all she has. After that, her options will have ended.

Which would be a relief.

For a coward.

But it hasn't been twenty-three minutes. Definitely not since the shooting. Probably not even since she walked into the bank.

Is Zoe a coward? She doesn't want to be. But she doesn't want to be dead, either. *Dead* is the end of all the possible stories of one's life. *Dead* is closing the choose-your-own-adventure book and returning it to the library—no, it's burning the book. *Dead* means no more chance for even having options.

I don't have to put my life in danger, Zoe tells herself. *I don't have to come back inside the bank. I can stop this from somewhere else.*

She hugs her arms tight around herself and makes the wish by saying, "Playback."

CHAPTER 4

TIME RESETS TO TWENTY-THREE MINUTES EARLIER.

Zoe is once again clutching her ill-gotten folder, back out on the street, closer to the hat and purse boutique—too cutely named Tops 'n Totes—than to the bank. It hasn't started raining yet, though the oddness of the light—unnaturally bright and glittery as the sunlight bounces off the dark and swollen-looking clouds—should be a warning to anyone who glances up at the sky. Zoe wonders how she could ever not have sought shelter at this point. Fortunately, a lot of other people don't have any more sense than she did.

To free her hands, she once more tucks her folder of papers beneath her t-shirt, securing it with the waistband of her jeans. If anyone on the street is alarmed to see that flash of her midriff, they're not saying.

She isn't used to asking for help and isn't quite sure of the best approach. She suspects if she sounds hysterical, this will scare people off; too composed, and they won't think twice about blowing her off.

"Excuse me," she says, almost grabbing for the arm of a woman passing by—but she hasn't lost herself that far, and knows touching would be a mistake.

Still, the woman practically recoils from Zoe. She is well dressed, probably a sales associate from one of the department stores, rushing to somewhere-or-other during her late lunch or her early-afternoon break. No doubt she has had experience with teenagers looking pretty much the way Zoe does. She has probably called store security on them.

Zoe camouflages her attempt to catch hold of the woman by swinging her arm around—rather dramatically, admittedly—and tapping her own wrist. Kind of a silly gesture, since most people check the time by looking at their cell phones and don't even own a wristwatch; but it gets the point across. Anyway, this woman is old enough that she probably has to ask her children when she wants to change her ringtones or add a new contact to her phone. She does have a watch, and she glances at it and, never quite stopping, never quite making eye contact with Zoe, says, "Quarter after."

"Excuse me," Zoe repeats, calling to the woman's back but not racing after her, which would likely cause the woman to drop dead from a heart attack. But such a nice round number sounds as though it comes from glancing at a clock face, not reporting a digital readout. "Is that the exact time? It's important."

The woman is still suspicious, and even glances around as though to make sure Zoe isn't with a gang, isn't trying to distract her before accomplices rush in to knock her down and grab her purse.

Is this woman *always* so skittish or is there something wrong with the way Zoe looks? Zoe glances down at herself, half expecting to see she's still spattered with blood, although that is not how things work when she plays back time.

"One seventeen," the woman says.

"Thank you." Zoe tries to sound genuinely grateful, without showing the dripping sugary sarcasm she really feels.

1:17. Well, subtract a minute for trying to get a straight answer out of her. It was probably 1:16 when Zoe arrived back here. So 1:16 (actual starting time) + 23 minutes (the fullest extent of playback) means Zoe has until 1:39 in what Zoe thinks of as flux time. Zoe has made up these terms herself, because there has never been anyone to explain these things to her. Of course not. Zoe is a freak, with a freakish talent. She suspects that in previous centuries her ability would have gotten her the reputation of being a witch. Zoe prefers to think of herself as a freak, rather than a witch. A freak who has the ability to play back life—twenty-three minutes at a time. Once she has started a playback, she can stop partway through and return to the same starting time—up to ten repeats if she so chooses—which is why she thinks of this time as being in flux. It isn't permanently set until the full twenty-three minutes are over. At which point, that particular twenty-three-minute segment of time—she thinks of it as a story line—solidifies? Closes off? In any case, that whole block of time is permanently no longer available to her fiddling. The story moves on . . .

But Zoe has no intention of *fiddling* with this playback. She has one easy goal—although for *that* her deadline is much shorter than twenty-three minutes. She probably wasted a good five minutes after the shooting, and there had to be six or seven minutes before that when the bank robber was already out of control.

Ten minutes, Zoe estimates. She has ten minutes to contact the police and warn them about a robbery in progress. Zoe doesn't especially like police. Being in the system, she has had several encounters with them and feels that the best of them are perhaps good-hearted but ineffectual, and the worst made the career choice to justify being bullies. Still, they're professionals. To be fair, they're probably better trained to deal with armed felons than with socially disadvantaged teens. The police should be able to prevent anyone from getting killed. And by *anyone*, she has in mind *customers* or even *bank staff*. She is not such an altruist as to be particularly concerned about a thief who would bring a gun into a bank and be prepared to use it.

She wipes her hands on her jeans, unable to rid herself of the sensation that they are speckled with the blood of two dead men. Even though she can see they are not.

Zoe looks around. From what she has heard, there *used* to be pay phones scattered throughout the city, available for those who needed to contact somebody before cell phones were invented. She supposes there probably still are pay phones somewhere, but she doesn't have time to search one out.

She sees a girl who looks about her own age, though Zoe suspects that, without makeup, she herself looks younger than she really is, perhaps closer to junior high than high school. Still, here's a girl who is probably about fifteen or sixteen, very chic in a short skirt and high heels that would never be good for a quick getaway—for whatever that's worth—and who is talking on a cell phone.

"Excuse me," Zoe says, falling into step next to her. "I don't have a phone and I absolutely need to make a call. It's an emergency. May I please borrow yours?"

The girl looks up at her as though she has never, ever, in her entire life, had anyone ask for such an outrageous favor. She tells the person at the other end of the call, "Just a sec," then says to Zoe, "I don't have, like, an unlimited plan."

"OK," Zoe counters. "But this is, like, literally life-and-death."

Without answering, the girl turns abruptly to enter a gift shop.

Zoe considers following her in, but decides against it. If the girl is frightened of her—or even just annoyed by her—and if she complains to the shopkeeper, there's no question with which of them the people in the shop will sympathize.

Instead, she looks around some more. There are a couple of young guys, wearing uniforms from a fast-food place, who are sitting on the edge of one of the huge sidewalk planters. They are talking and texting and laughing, but Zoe dismisses them because there is always *such* a chance of misunderstanding where guys are concerned. Similarly, she doesn't give serious consideration to the grandfatherly guy walking the big dog that looks as though it could eat small children for a snack, or to the biker guy who has a Chihuahua at the end of *his* leash. She spots a woman walking with a girl and a boy, both preteens, and she zeroes in on them.

"Hello," she says, "I'm sorry to bother you—but, please, I need help." *Bad choice of words*, she reprimands herself, even as they're coming out of her mouth. What if the woman thinks she's asking for money? She should have thought this out beforehand. Hurriedly she adds, "Do you have a phone I could please, please, please use? It's really important. A local call. It won't take a minute. Please." She hates groveling but figures her pride is less important than a life.

The boy, who looks all of about eleven, demands, "Why don't you have your own phone?" and the mother drapes her arm around his shoulders in what might be a case of oh-isn't-my-boy-the-most-precious-thing-ever pride, or might be gentle chastisement. Zoe's own mother, whom she hasn't seen in almost two years, was never gentle with her chastisements. Meanwhile, the little girl reaches over to clutch her mother's free hand. Clearly, Zoe makes her nervous. Clearly, this child has had impressed on her the dangers of speaking to strangers.

Still, Zoe hopes the mother is thinking that should her own children ever be in trouble, some friendly soul would be willing to help them. And, in fact, the woman digs a phone out of her purse and, though somewhat reluctantly, hands it to Zoe.

Zoe stares at it for a moment before the woman explains, "Press the green button, then the numbers you need."

It isn't that the phone is too complicated to figure out: Zoe has been distracted by noting the time—1:22. Assuming the first woman was right, Zoe has squandered only five minutes. There's still plenty of time.

Except at that exact moment, the sky opens up. Zoe, the woman, and the children rush to huddle under the nearest store's awning. The woman sighs, no doubt already regretting the generous impulse that has left her and her kids standing in the rain with this phone-borrowing stranger.

Zoe presses the green button, then 911.

Whether the woman can see which numbers Zoe has pressed or guesses by how few have been pressed, she raises her eyebrows, looking a bit apprehensive.

"911," the dispatcher announces. "What number are you calling from?"

Why do they always ask that? Zoe wonders. She knows for a fact that the number has shown up on their equipment. She knows this from the time when Rasheena and Delia were arguing, while Mrs. Davies was in the kitchen, and Delia grabbed the phone and hit 911 before one of the other girls was able to get the phone back and hang up. But still, two minutes later, someone from 911 called back to see what the emergency was. And even dispatched a police car, despite the fact that everyone—including Delia—said, "Oops. Never mind. Mistake." Mrs. Davies had not been amused.

So now the dispatcher has asked for the number, and Zoe says, "I don't know. I'm calling from somebody else's cell phone. Do you need me to find out?"

"No, that's all right," the man on the other end of the line says. "What's your emergency?"

Zoe takes a deep breath. "I saw a man with a gun. Entering Spencerport Savings and Loan on Independence Street."

The woman whose phone she's borrowed throws a protective arm around each of her children, even though Independence Street is two and a half blocks away, and the bank is halfway down the block after turning the corner.

"No, I'm not in the bank," Zoe answers when the dispatcher asks. In response to his next question, she tries to remember what the man looked like. "I don't know. Forty, fifty." Old people are old; how is she supposed to be able to tell *how* old? "White guy . . . no, I couldn't see his hair. He had a hoodie and a baseball cap . . . tan raincoat . . . taller than me,"—which is ridiculous since the dispatcher can't know how tall she is—"shorter than . . ."

She cuts herself off. She was thinking that he was a bit shorter than the guy he ended up killing. She remembers how the thief's arm was angled up to press against the young man's throat, pinning him against the wall, the gun against his temple . . . She once again feels the spatter of the warm blood against her face and chest, and she can't stop her free hand from reaching up to her hair, to feel for the bits that have lodged themselves there.

Zoe starts shaking and can't talk anymore. She cuts off the connection halfway through something-or-other the 911 dispatcher is saying and holds the phone back out to the woman with the kids.

"Is that true?" the boy demands, sounding like a district attorney cross-examining a hostile witness. Obviously, this child's mother has let him watch way too much TV. "You came all the way here from Independence Street before you could find *anybody* to let you borrow their phone?"

"Sherman, hush," the mother says, taking the phone. But she once again glances back in the direction of Independence.

The phone rings. Well, actually, it plays the theme from the Indiana Jones movies. The woman sees the calling number and holds the phone out to Zoe.

Zoe shakes her head and takes a step away.

The woman's face immediately grows red enough that she looks ready to burst. "You better not have used my phone to make a crank call," she practically spits out.

"I didn't," Zoe protests. "I saw him. He—"

The boy interrupts. "And he let you leave during the actual robbery? Or did he take the gun out on the street for all the world to see and *then* walk into the bank?"

"No," Zoe says. "I . . ." But her voice drifts off. How can she possibly answer? Telling people about playback has caused more problems than playback itself.

The boy continues in his scornful tone: "And he didn't even wear a mask to hide his face?"

Zoe pictures it again: How the man shot out the cameras that would have left a record, as though not concerned about the human witnesses. The moment when Zoe had the realization that he was going to kill them all. When she would have played back, except he was holding onto her at the time.

"No," Zoe tries to explain. "But he had a hoodie. And his collar up. And . . ."

The obnoxious kid is sneering, unwilling to believe the most believable aspect of her story.

"There was a man with a gun," Zoe repeats. "In Spencerport Savings and Loan. And I can't simply dawdle"—*dawdle* was one of her mother's words—"around here and *chat* with you."

She turns on her heel and steps back out into the rain, walking rapidly away from them, away—even more so—from Independence Street and the bank that is about to be held up

"Hey!" the woman calls after her. "Hey!" The Indiana Jones theme, which had stopped briefly, starts again.

Zoe begins running, despite the rain-slickness of the sidewalk.

She turns down Franklin and makes another turn when she gets to Valencia. The woman can't conceivably be chasing after her. The boy on his own might—probably would, in best cop show tradition—but not the mother. Definitely not the mother with the timid little girl in tow. Zoe just hopes they won't talk the 911 people out of believing her call.

She stops to readjust the folder, which is digging into her side, which is when she starts to hear sirens. *Good*, she thinks. Though surely the police wouldn't approach a bank robbery with their sirens blaring, alerting the robber, would they? And yet the noise seems to be coming from behind her, in the general vicinity of the bank.

None of your business, she reminds herself yet again.

She has to have been in this story line at least seventeen, eighteen minutes by now.

Twenty-three, and it will be irrevocably lost.

She hopes the one guy—the one who, in this particular twenty-three-minute interval, she has not met, so who has not been kind to her—she hopes he has managed to not get himself killed this time. And she tries to avoid picturing all that blood on the wall behind where he'd been standing. That blood. And hair . . .

None of your damn business, she mentally yells at herself.

Leave well enough alone.

Ooh, that's one of Mrs. Davies's sayings.

Perhaps because of that, she does the opposite thing: She starts running back down Valencia. Past Franklin, past North Main, past Academy. Independence is the next cross street, and she sees police cars have it blocked off.

Gawkers are pressed against the barricade, but Zoe pushes through the crowd. Police cars are all over the area. Ambulances, and even a fire truck, are at the ready farther back. At the ready for what, exactly? Police in full protective gear are crouched behind any cover they can get, holding an impressive array of impressive weapons. There's glass on the street, the front window from the bank shattered from the inside out. There's also a body—no, two—on the street, and one on the sidewalk.

Once again, she wipes the shadow of blood from her hands.

"What happened?" Zoe's nearly breathless from her run, and her words come out barely a whisper.

"Hostage situation in the bank," someone tells her. There's

always someone eager to share bad news. "Lots of shots fired. Including through the window, out into the street, as the police were arriving."

The man points to the body on the sidewalk, outlined in a pool of blood. "Lady," he says, "pushing a stroller."

Oh no oh no oh no.

Zoe finally notices the stroller, tipped on its side. At least the toddler strapped inside is kicking his legs, the only encouraging sign at this scene.

"That guy," the witness continues, pointing, "was only a passerby trying to help. Other one's police."

His voice is drowned out by the *whup-whup-whup* of a helicopter overhead.

What's going on *inside* the bank? With the gunman shooting out into the street, surely that's an indication the bank guard, at least, is dead. So . . . three for sure dead on the street. Almost certainly at least one dead inside. And probably others. The guy with the jacket? No telling.

What have I done? Zoe thinks. This is even worse than before. She should have known. Only rarely has she had good luck with going back and trying to change what has happened—and then it's usually been only with small one-variable things, like knowing to untuck the hem of her skirt from her waistband before leaving the restroom instead of *after* walking into a courtroom full of people for her shelter hearing, the day she was removed from her parents' home.

The witness beside her is trying to draw something-or-other to her attention, even though the noise of the helicopter prevents her from hearing his words. Her gaze strays to his cell phone—he has been recording the goings-on, but she can see the time displayed on the screen. Just a few seconds short of 1:39. The twenty-three minutes is almost—if not already—over.

But if it isn't . . .

She can't leave things like this. She *has* to try.

Yeah, she thinks. *If I keep this up, maybe I can start a nuclear holocaust.*

But she hugs herself and says, "Playback."

And apparently the twenty-three minutes were not quite over, because Zoe finds herself back in front of the hat and purse boutique.

CHAPTER 5

Time resets to 1:16.

It is not yet raining.

The robber is not yet inside the bank.

Nobody is dead.

Zoe wipes the memory of blood off her palms onto the thighs of her jeans.

OK, so obviously calling the police somehow caused the situation to escalate totally out of control. *Being there* was bad, *calling the police* was worse. Should she not do anything? She thinks again of the customer who stepped in to rescue her. In the absence of a name, she's beginning to think of him as The Boy Scout. And not entirely in a complimentary way. But the thing is: He had no particular reason to protect *her*. She suspects he's the kind of person with not enough sense to keep himself from getting killed all over again in a situation like this. For Zoe, simply *not seeing it happen* is not a solution.

Once again she tucks her folder into her waistband and begins to run toward Independence Street. In the original story line, she was meandering, nowhere to go, no set time to be anyplace, knowing she would be facing detention when she got back to the group home; so she'd been pausing to look in shop windows to admire all the things other people could have—or even just hope to have. That took her six minutes. She now knows this from the fact that she was looking at the cell phone clock this last time just as the rain started.

She passes by the mother with her two children. The boy is tugging on the mother's arm, and both children are whining to go into the candy shop. While the mother is explaining the evils of refined sugar and of ruining one's supper, Zoe fights the juvenile inclination to stick out her tongue at all of them.

As she runs, she tries to remember the sequence of events, who came in when. Boy Scout must have been in the bank already, since his clothing was not wet. She can't picture where he might have been standing: Pouring himself a cup of that complimentary coffee? In the vault-like room where safety deposit boxes line the walls? In the sitting area waiting to talk to one of the important bank managers who have little offices of their own, where they discuss opening or closing accounts, getting loans, and whatever else bank people talk about when customers want privacy? Truth be told, the bank was fairly busy, and she hadn't noticed him until she backed into him. And that happened after the man who would turn out to be the robber practically plowed into her when *he* came into the bank. When, exactly, would that have been?

But none of that is important at this point—or at least Zoe hopes it isn't.

She slows down a few steps short of the entrance so as not to be running near the bank, which she instinctively recognizes might potentially be a suspicion-arousing thing.

Still, the running and the nervousness have left her out of breath as she pushes open the bank door.

The bank guard is just as displeased to have her walk through that door dry as he was to see her come in wet. He obviously perceives her as trouble.

Finely honed sense of who bears watching, Zoe reflects, knowing the armed bank robber will pass the guard's scrutiny.

Still, she approaches the guard, because that is what she's come here to do.

"Excuse me," she says, even though she already has his attention.

He nods, the barest minimum civil response.

"I need to speak with you."

No response at all to that. By which, on reflection, she takes him to mean: *Well . . . clearly you already ARE speaking to me. And I am not yet beating you away with a stick, though I reserve that option . . .*

Life is so much simpler when you don't have to talk to people.

She says, "There's a suspicious man . . ." She is thinking, *This is not going to work.* She should leave now. Not look back.

Not watch the news tonight.

Or for the next couple days.

Why is she always jumping into things?

The guard asks, "Suspicious in what way?" His eyes narrow. "Has someone been bothering you?"

It takes Zoe a moment to realize what he's asking.

And in that moment, the guard seems to have second thoughts. He's taking into account the look of her, with her blue ponytail coming loose from its elastic, her clunky combat boots, and her t-shirt (old to start with, even by thrift-store standards, and now lumpy from the folder beneath it, not to mention sweat-spotted from her running, despite the coolness of the day). The shirt says "Guns N' Roses," which she assumes was a rock band from somewhere near the dawn of time, and she wonders if the guard's memory goes back far enough to know who they were, or if he's simply thinking it's bad form for anyone to walk into a bank with a shirt that has "Guns" written on it. She guesses he's realized she's older than he thought at first glance, and that he's thinking: *Who would ever bother HER?* And, in fact, he modifies his earlier question by asking, "Has some stranger been bothering you?" Like: *Of course you have scary acquaintances, and I don't want to get involved in that.*

Zoe says, "No. But . . . I think there might be somebody planning to rob the bank."

"Excuse me?" the guard says frostily, not sounding convinced. Sounding pretty much the exact opposite of convinced.

"I saw a man with a gun . . ."

This is a mistake, because the guard demands, "Where?" and Zoe doesn't know from which direction the robber is going to approach.

She glances back over her shoulder, looks left and right, and in that movement clearly loses all credibility with the guard.

"Ha, ha," he says. "Very funny. Except making a false report can get you in serious trouble."

"No," Zoe says. "Really. He's going to rob the bank—"

But the guard has taken hold of her upper arm, and he is moving her—somewhere between not gently and not roughly—to the door. Talking with her is so important to him that he takes the time to hold the door open for someone else, a woman who is leaving the bank. "Have a nice day," the guard tells the woman, proving he can be pleasant after all. Just not to Zoe.

"*Really*," Zoe repeats.

But the guard cuts her off again. "Yeah, *really*," he says. "Stuff like that can *really* get you in trouble." He's still holding the door open even though the woman has stepped outside, because someone else is coming in.

For a second, Zoe doesn't even recognize the customer who may well have saved her life, and it isn't until he removes his sunglasses as he steps indoors that she sees it's Jacket, aka Boy Scout. Well, the first thing she sees is that the sunglasses probably cost more than her entire outfit, not that she feels sorry for herself or anything. Then she sees that, apparently, he only responds to clumsy girls who step on him and drop papers with reindeer names at his feet—which the people at the group home would probably call An Issue—because he's looking down at his own envelope of papers, and he doesn't even see her or that she is being officially escorted from the bank.

The guard finally releases her arm. "You, young lady, could get in serious trouble for that kind of nonsense. Do yourself a favor and knock it off. If you've got friends watching in the hope of seeing me get all flustered, tell them to knock it off, too."

He pulls the door shut between them.

Now what?

Zoe presses her face against the window in time to note Boy Scout going into one of the offices that border the waiting area. Probably seeing about a loan to afford his expensive clothes.

The guard raps his knuckles against the glass, making her jump. Once he has her attention, he points at a "No Loitering" sign.

At which instant the rain starts.

Of course it does. She thinks of it as heaven spitting on her.

What now? Zoe hopes she has put a suspicion in the guard's head. Not about herself. *That* she knows she has accomplished. But about a robbery. She hopes the guard will take a closer look at the people coming into the bank. That he will notice how the twitchy man with the big raincoat is hiding his face. And his hands.

And that, being prepared, the guard will be able to do something before the situation gets out of control.

Zoe crosses the street and stands in the doorway of the card shop. Only half out of the rain, but positioned so she can see up and down both sides of the street.

One of the card shop clerks, a girl who looks only marginally older than Zoe, holds the door open as a middle-aged customer scurries out into the rain, carrying a package and a breeze of the store's scented candles and potpourri with her.

Zoe must look very pathetic—either that or business is incredibly slow today—because the clerk calls out to Zoe, "Why don't you come on in out of the wet?"

"Thank you," Zoe says. "I'm waiting for someone." She figures it's best not to mention that the person she's waiting for is a sociopathic murderer.

As though to help her with this waiting-for-someone alibi, a car pulls up directly in front of the card shop. Just as Zoe is mentally urging the driver to move on one further parking space so as not to block her view, she catches a flash of red as he places a Red Wings baseball cap on his head, then pulls up the collar of his tan raincoat before getting out of the car.

She could rush out of the doorway and try to trip him. But she's not convinced:

a) that this would deflect him from his intention of armed robbery, or

b) that he wouldn't be annoyed enough at her to take out his gun and shoot her, or even

44

c) that he couldn't easily walk around her.

As the would-be bank robber crosses the street, Zoe flings open the door to the card shop and shouts, "Did you see that? That man has a gun! He's walking into the bank! Someone call 911!"

There are two clerks: the girl who took pity on Zoe's wet state and an older man. There's also a woman customer wearing hair rollers, who has been looking at the display of area attraction memorabilia: mugs and caps and teddy bears with I ♥ *Rochester, NY* t-shirts. (Who wears hair rollers anymore? And who buys souvenirs of Rochester, NY?) They all seem to take her seriously, with the two women engaging in some high-pitched fluttering, and the guy picking up the phone behind the counter.

The time is slightly later than when Zoe made the call from in front of Tops 'n Totes two blocks away. And it's a respectable sounding older man making the call. Will this somehow make a difference?

There's nothing more she can accomplish here. Well, nothing *good*, Zoe thinks. There's always the potential of these people taking a closer look at her, deciding she's not to be trusted, telling the police, "Never mind." It's better to leave before any of that can happen.

"I'm going to check his license plate," Zoe announces.

"No!" the male clerk shouts at her, thinking only too late to cover the phone receiver in consideration of the 911 dispatcher's eardrum. "It's safer in here. Valerie, go lock the door. All of you, come back here behind the counter."

The young clerk, Valerie, clearly feels she's already too close to the door, and that the man with the gun who's been spotted on the street might have second thoughts about robbing the bank and choose at any moment to turn back and take on the card shop instead. Her wide, terrified gaze shifts between the door and the counter, and she remains exactly where she is, her feet rooted to the floor.

Zoe could grab one of the light-up musical pens from the display to record the license plate number on the back of her hand, or on the folder which is still tucked safely beneath her shirt. But she seriously doubts things will ever resolve themselves in a way that the police will be trying to track this guy down. She might need the number if she's to play back this story line, this twenty-three-minute interval, but if so, she will start—yet again—at 1:16, in front of the hat and purse boutique, dry and numberless, exactly as she was the first time she passed through 1:16. Only her memories will have changed.

Mostly what she wants is an excuse to be out on the sidewalk, even though everyone in the card shop most assuredly thinks this is a bad idea.

Ignoring their protests, Zoe steps outside and to the back of the car. HDP 347. She memorizes the letters by assigning them a mnemonic: Highly Deranged Person. Zoe isn't very adept at numbers, but tries to commit 347 to memory.

She is aware of the woman with the hair rollers tapping on the glass of the store door, trying to motion Zoe back in. The sound is reminiscent of the bank guard knocking on the window and indicating for her to move on, but these people are concerned for her safety, and that makes Zoe feel twinge-y in all sorts of ways.

But, despite the way she's standing behind the robber's car so her new friends won't become suspicious of her and let that suspicion overflow into the conversation with 911, despite that,

46

what she's really doing is making sure she can see into the bank through the bank's big plate-glass window.

The robber walks in.

The guard whom Zoe warned is no longer distracted by Zoe's shenanigans at the table for the deposit/withdrawal slips, and is busy chatting up an attractive woman in her twenties and doesn't even notice the robber.

But the other person Zoe isn't there to distract, Boy Scout, *he* sees. And does he go about his own business, or—noticing something is wrong about the man—very sensibly get out of there, or sound an alarm, or do any other prudent thing? No, of course he doesn't.

In a moment, too fast to tell exactly what's happened, not without being able to hear, there's a confrontation between the two of them. The robber pulls out his gun. Shoots Boy Scout. Shoots the guard. Shoots the attractive twenty-something. Shoots one of the tellers.

Crap crap crap, Zoe thinks.

On the street, she notices an oblivious young woman pushing a baby stroller at top speed to get out of the rain, making a dash for her car, parked directly in front of the bank.

"Man with a gun!" Zoe screams at her.

The woman skids to a stop.

One life. One life saved.

Zoe hears more shooting from inside the bank.

She puts her arms around herself and whispers, "Playback."

CHAPTER 6

T IME RESETS TO 1:16.

Standing in front of Tops 'n Totes, Zoe considers her options.

All right. So it's no use having someone call the police from the card shop once the robber makes his entrance. That's too late to have an effect on anything: of itself, neither a good decision nor a bad one.

Letting the robber walk in while she watches from the safety of outside . . . that definitely comes under the heading of *bad* decision. It resulted in four deaths right away. And he was still firing his gun when she played back time.

That's right up there with her first playback.

Zoe tries to back away from the thought that the original twenty-three minutes—the original story line—involved the fewest number of people getting killed: just the gunman, and one victim. Forget calling him Jacket or Boy Scout; she's beginning to think of him as the reincarnation of the premier bad-luck president, William Henry Harrison, who couldn't make it through an inauguration without catching his death of a chill. Her guy can't make it through a bank robbery.

I can't choose who's to die, Zoe protests to herself. She's always hated those morality questions thought up by philosophers and psychologists who want to torment their students and/or patients:

If the whole village can be happy at the cost of one child's life, is that child's life worth it? What if the whole village can be happy at the cost of two children's lives? What if . . . ?

What kind of stupid-ass question is that? Zoe asked in sociology class. (A required course, or she would never have been taking it.) *If the villagers are so damn happy, why can't they find a way to accommodate one frigging kid?*

She'd gotten a failing mark for that particular essay. As well as a stern talking-to.

Now here she is with that one theoretical child on *her* hands.

It doesn't help that he's no longer theoretical. She's met him. Admired his hair, his smile, his kindness. His ability to name all Santa's reindeer. He is, for all intents and purposes, William Henry Harrison, Junior. She determines that this is a most suitable name, and this is what she'll call him. She sifts amongst William, Will, Bill, and Junior before settling on Mr. President.

She doesn't want to go back to that original twenty-three minutes. She doesn't want Mr. President to die, nor does she want to weigh how many lives she would consider his to be worth. Besides everything else, she is totally aware that all it would take would be one little slip on her part, one thing done slightly differently, and she herself might end up getting killed. No way to play back from that. She also reflects on how Mr. President stopped to be kind to her *inside* the bank, yet didn't even notice her this last time, when she'd been confronting the guard in the doorway.

Not that this means she wants to throw him under the wheels of the robbery bus.

The housemother she used to have, the one before Mrs. Davies, used to complain that Zoe was too impatient and rushed into situations without thinking things through. Like the time Zoe sprained her ankle and the doctor told her to keep off it for forty-eight hours. But she got bored after a day and went out with her friends, making the injury worse so that she ended up being confined to the infirmary for a week. Or like when she'd been grounded after she borrowed (yes, it was without asking, but she fully intended to return it) the ID of one of the younger-looking social workers in an attempt to convince a tattoo artist she was eighteen. Or when she was too eager to move into her newly painted room and didn't wait as long as she'd been told to before hauling her stuff back in—resulting in a streak of white on the seat of her jeans and a butt-shaped smudge on her wall where you could see through to the old puke-green color. "Heedless of the future," this particular housemother used to intone, in the solemn voice of someone speaking from the pulpit.

But this time Zoe *is* planning ahead. She needs to replay the original story line—but only up to a point. *This time*, she tells herself, *I'll know what's coming. I can be standing farther from the teller counter. I can try to keep everybody safe. I can draw the guard's attention to the robber right away.*

I will not be an idle bystander.

She'd been an idle bystander with her parents at the Counseling Center when she was thirteen, and she had promised herself then that she would never again be so useless.

Exactly how she'll accomplish all this, she doesn't know, but the key will be to make sure Mr. President is at a farther distance from the robber. She hopes this will keep him out of harm's way and, by extension, will keep the others in the bank from becoming victims of the robber's ire.

One more try, she tells herself.

This will be it, no matter what. Mr. President, nice smile and all, has to take his chances.

She looks at the folder she's once again holding, the folder she'd thought—only this morning—that she had risked all to get her hands on. She mentally snorts at herself: She'd had no idea what *all* was.

But she's not yet willing to part with it. This will be her last go-around, she promises herself. Besides, apparently she needs these papers to get Mr. President's attention.

The woman who'd told her the time in the first playback makes a wide detour around her, bumping into the teenage girl who is still too busy talking on her phone to be aware of anything else.

Zoe passes the other woman, the one with the two kids, as they're leaving the candy store. *Pushover*, Zoe thinks at the mother scornfully, before she sees that they haven't bought candy—they've stopped to put a donation in the jar to raise money for muscular dystrophy. This is unexpected.

Not that this causes her to like them any better or anything.

She walks faster than she did the first time, to make up for dallying while trying to decide what to do.

But she's overcompensated, because when she gets to the bank, the rain hasn't started yet. Should she go in even though she's a minute or so early? What possible repercussions could that have? And would they necessarily be bad?

Silly question, she chides herself. *Of course they'd be bad.*

On the other hand, she is also concerned about hanging around outside the bank door. Will the guard notice and be even more suspicious of her? And what bad thing could *that* lead to? Is the robber watching the place, and will his suspicions be aroused?

Ooh, she thinks, *that might actually be a good thing.* He might decide to postpone his robbery until some other day, or he might choose another bank. She couldn't possibly be responsible for people under those circumstances.

Which is the point at which nature steps in and empties a sky-full of rainwater onto her.

Zoe dutifully shoves the folder under her Guns N' Roses t-shirt and enters.

The guard scowls at her, a look like he's bitten down into what he thought was a fluffy piece of sugar candy but turned out to be a lemon-flavored rock.

Obviously there's no way she will ever be anything other than a source of irritation to him.

She heads for the table with the deposit/withdrawal slips, then remembers that the first time, she took the folder out from under her shirt before going there.

She takes it out now, but worries that things are already irrevocably wrong.

Uh-huh. How much more wrong can you get than intentionally placing yourself in the path of a bank robber with a proven track record of killing indiscriminately?

Zoe moves to the table and takes a form. Pink is for deposits, she notices this time; white for withdrawals. She uses some of each and writes down the names of Santa's reindeer. She knows she made other lists before but can't remember what they were, so she just goes ahead and makes several copies of the same one. This time, thanks to Mr. President's previous intervention, she has all nine names.

As she's watching the people lining up for the tellers, she wonders if she's spending too much time looking at them, and if that is making the guard more suspicious than the first time. Her gaze wanders—despite her best intentions—to the office where Mr. President is currently sitting talking to one of the managers. *Probably not asking for a loan*, she decides; he looks too relaxed to be begging. She settles on the theory that he's investing a sum of money he inherited from a maiden aunt—he was no doubt her favorite nephew.

She forces herself to stop staring and speculating. She worries she's spent too long gawking in a direction she never even noticed before.

The last person in the tellers' line at the moment is the same woman with the pointy-toed shoes whom Zoe believes she stood behind last time.

So Zoe gets in line. Has the same non-conversation with the same teller about presidential coins in general and William Henry Harrison—the Original—in particular. Once again, the teller looks resentful that she needs to play nice and pretend she considers Zoe a valued customer.

Finished with that, Zoe goes off to the side and stands at the forms table again.

This time she's aware of Mr. President coming out of the office with his envelope of papers, which he puts down beside her as he reaches for one of the deposit slips.

Through the main entrance, Zoe sees the robber get out of his car and sprint across the street.

How could she have not noticed, before, that his face is very suspiciously just-about-entirely obscured?

Previously, the bank guard did not believe her when she said a robber was about to enter the bank. Her plan this time is to wait until the robber is at the counter. Then she will run over and tell the guard, "Look! That guy has a gun." Hopefully the guard will not blow her off once he actually sees the man.

For now, Zoe intentionally steps backward—fortunately finding Mr. President's foot right away, so she doesn't have to be obvious with multiple tries. She flings her folder of papers in the general direction of his knees.

"Sorry," she says before he can get a word out. "Sorry. I am *such* an idiot."

She fervently hopes she hasn't made *him* suspicious of her, just because she's trying to get him down on the floor a few seconds early.

But apparently not.

"These things happen to everyone," he assures her.

They both crouch down and scramble for the papers. Even though Zoe has angled herself differently, to be able to keep watch on the counter behind which the tellers are positioned, this time she and Mr. President manage to collect all the papers from the group home and all the bank slips quickly enough that the guard doesn't come over. Zoe wonders what disaster that will precipitate.

Neither Zoe nor Mr. President has stood yet. Zoe is aware that he is looking closely at her, scrutinizing. Did he do that before?

She can't be sure and, in any case, pretends not to notice as she aligns the papers to fit them back into the folder.

He asks, quiet and gentle, "Are you all right?"

Which is new, but doesn't sound dangerous.

"Yeah, sure," she says, even as the front door opens, letting in the soon-to-be robber on a blast of cold, rainy air.

Mr. President is watching her, and the bank guard is watching both of them. Neither notices the man with the raincoat and the cap, and the bulkiness in his right-hand pocket.

Mr. President asks Zoe, "Truly?"

Truly? Zoe thinks. Who actually says *truly*? She believes the only time she's ever used the word *truly* was when her language arts teacher had the class practice writing what she called "friendly" letters (as opposed to "business" letters, not as opposed to "unfriendly" letters), some of which ended with *Sincerely*, and others, *Yours truly*.

"Yeah," she repeats to Mr. President. "Truly." She glances at him just in time to see him stealing a look down at her hands, holding one of the Santa's reindeer sheets. He's holding one, too, except his is on a pink form, while hers is on white. *Ah!* she thinks, too late. *I shouldn't have included Blitzen.* Now they have nothing to talk about. By way of explanation, she offers, "It's been a very rough day." Her voice unexpectedly quavers, like she's talking into an electric fan.

He looks up at that exact moment, and their eyes meet.

The breath she's been trying to steady catches. Because they're crouching on the floor so close to each other without him standing taller than she is, or because of some trick of the lighting, or because of . . . of something . . .

Has she ever seen bluer eyes? How could she not have noticed them before? She was looking directly into his eyes when . . . when . . . yeah, leave it at *before*. She remembers vaguely noting that they were blue, and that they seemed to hold equal measures of being scared and being brave. But she did not note the striking color.

The only trouble is that remembering the moment right before the gunman pulled the trigger is abruptly followed by remembering the moment right after.

She winces, her face and arms once again feeling flicked by his blood.

Mr. President looks alarmed. Even touches the back of her hand with his fingertips. "Do you need help? Is there someone I can call?"

That would be one *yes* and one *no*.

And she can no longer bear to think of him in connection with the ill-fated William Henry Harrison.

For him, the next words out of her mouth must sound bizarrely appropriate to absolutely nothing: "What's your name?" she asks.

He looks startled, but doesn't demand *Why?* Though her question clearly puzzles him, he answers, "Daniel."

She likes that he says Daniel, not Dan or Danny—not that it makes any difference or that it's any of her business. She says, "I want to thank you, Daniel."

Her intensity has him looking even more mystified, and just the slightest bit worried.

"For your kindness," she clarifies, which—in the interval they're currently living—clarifies nothing.

He's still frowning in concentration, trying to follow, and she's thinking that her earlier assessment—more interesting than attractive—was way off. She'd thought before that he had a great smile. Now she's thinking that his looks as a whole are growing on her.

Which is downright ridiculous, because he's still too old for her.

Not to mention that they're still in a bank that's about to get shot up by a robber.

Just as she's thinking that, one of the tellers squeals in alarm.

I was supposed to have been watching HIM, Zoe chides herself: the man she knew had come here to rob the bank. Not Daniel.

Still, she's able to catch up in a heartbeat. At this moment, there are seven other customers in the bank, none waiting in line. The robber is in front of the teller, the one who does not have any William Henry Harrison coins, the one who looked pissed off at having to wait on Zoe, little suspecting then that waiting on Zoe would turn out to be the least of her problems.

The next teller over, the one at the station to the extreme right, has just slid a lumpy canvas bag over to her. Zoe can see there are stacks of money packed inside, and a piece of paper lying on top, no doubt a *Hand over the money or die* note. By squealing rather than quietly and efficiently filling the bag and then passing it on its way down the line, the second teller has alerted everyone in the room that something is very seriously amiss.

The robber pulls his right hand fully out of his pocket, revealing the gun.

Out of the corner of her eye, Zoe is aware of Daniel. Still crouched on the floor after helping her to pick up her papers, he has taken all this in. She can tell—maybe feeling it through that lightest touch of his fingertips on the back of her hand, maybe just because she can tell—that he's about to move, to do something in a misguided attempt to help. There's no time to warn him not to try a foolhardy intervention.

There's barely time for her to catch hold of the cuff of his jacket, to try to hold him back, away from harm.

His eyes shift to her, which gives her the moment she needs to whisper, "Don't. You'll only get killed."

He could take it as a panicky it's-always-better-not-to-get-involved response.

But she doesn't think he does.

Of course, there's no way for him to guess that she actually *knows* he'll get killed if he intervenes, but he hesitates, apparently choosing watchfulness over action, at least for this instant.

The officious bank guard, who has been paying close enough attention to Zoe and Daniel that he has not gotten distracted by the attractive twenty-something, is standing closer to the teller counter than before. "Hey!" he says, and moves his hand toward his gun.

The robber shoots him.

And Daniel proves he's terrible at staying on the sidelines and doing nothing. He lunges forward, slipping out of Zoe's grasp. Somehow, still barely more upright than in a crouch, he has once again gotten himself positioned between Zoe and the gunman.

Who shoots a second time.

Daniel falls back against her, knocking her down off her knees and onto her bottom.

He's gasping, having a hard time catching his breath, and Zoe puts a steadying arm around him, despite the nearly overpowering smell of blood, despite the massive wet stickiness she feels on his chest. *Please let him keep breathing*, she thinks to God, because surely a chest wound is better than a head wound. People can survive being shot in the chest.

Sometimes.

Her father did.

But meanwhile she's distracted because she's also thinking that, yeah, Daniel is an adult guy, but he's not all *that* big. And yet, Zoe feels as though she's been slammed into by . . . well, the image that comes to her mind is a freight train, not that she's ever been run into by a freight train, but she's certain it must feel like this.

So that is what Zoe is thinking as Daniel falls backward onto her, except the pain is centered on her upper left chest near her shoulder. *Heart attack?* she wonders, remembering having heard somewhere that severe pain in the left shoulder or upper arm is a warning sign.

Not for fifteen-year-old girls, though.

She looks down at herself and sees that she's once more covered with Daniel's blood.

Her head feels as though someone has stuffed it with a collection of pins, all trying to work their way out through her skull. And for some reason the pins seem to be humming as they work their way through brain and bone. Very Zen. Even so, she's aware of her surroundings, and that the robber is continuing his spree by shooting the attractive twenty-something, as well as Ms. No-I-have-no-William-Henry-Harrison-coins-bank-teller.

But for some reason the whole bank is tipping. Except, no—it's Zoe who's tipping. And she looks down again at her bloody shirt—Guns N' Roses, indeed—before she realizes that some of the blood is her own.

A lot of it is her own.

The bullet has gone through Daniel and into her.

And she's about to pass out.

She can no longer hear Daniel's raspy breathing. He has slumped forward. He might be unconscious, or he might be dead, or maybe it's just that the humming in her own head has gotten too loud. With no time to even check whether Daniel is alive, she shoves him off her. Kicks herself away, using his body as leverage. What kind of monster is she for even being able to do this? She hates herself, because it seems that a better person should be paralyzed by empathy for the young man she had hoped to save. But she can't playback her way out of here while touching anyone else. She knows this from experimenting when she was thirteen.

She wraps her arms around herself.

Sees the gunman's attention has been attracted by her movement.

He aims the gun at her.

She says, "Playback," but can't hear her own voice over the roar of the gun.

CHAPTER 7

TIME RESETS TO 1:16.

Zoe has just gone from sitting on the floor in the bank to standing—in front of the hat and purse boutique, of course.

She's also just been shot. Twice, she suspects.

Still, the bullets, the wounds, have not traveled back in time with her. Because that's just not the way things work: Nothing *ever* travels back with her, only her memories—her damn memories.

It wasn't that long ago that she was thinking she'd just come as close as she ever had to dying, and now here she is again, having come even closer.

This is not a personal best record she ever wants to visit again.

Whatever else happens, there's one thing in the world she absolutely knows will *not*: She will not go back into that bank.

Off-balance, she teeters and falls to her knees, not sure if she's fallen from the sudden shift from sitting to standing as time played back, or by the realization of how very, very, very close she came to getting killed. Or by the thought that she has no more left to give. She cannot bring herself to go back. Surely no one—God, the universe, even Daniel himself—could expect her to try again after that.

One way or another, Daniel will die within the next twenty-three minutes, and probably a whole bunch of other people will, too.

All she's accomplished is to get to know Daniel a little bit better than simply as the sweet, nameless bank customer who died within moments of being kind to her.

It's not fair, it's not fair, she thinks, covering her face. She doesn't want him to die; she doesn't want herself to die.

Someone has laid a hand on her shoulder. "Miss," a voice says. "Hon. You all right?"

Not Daniel's voice.

Never again Daniel's voice.

Zoe looks up.

The biker guy walking his Chihuahua has stopped and is leaning down to look at her with a solicitous expression. The Chihuahua is yapping at her, dragging its leash through the folder and the papers that are littering the ground around her knees, doing an excellent job of shuffling and spreading them.

After what's just happened, it's hard to be concerned about that.

She hears the biker guy answer someone, "I don't know. She just fell. I was looking right at her, but I didn't see what happened."

A small crowd has gathered. The department store saleswoman, the one who once told her the time, slows but does not stop.

The girl with the cell phone that does not have unlimited minutes asks, "Is she all right? Should I call 911?"

"No!" Zoe practically screams at her.

Everyone freezes, except for glancing at each other from the corners of their eyes. *See that?* everyone seems to be silently asking. *Oh yeah*, everyone mentally answers. *Don't let her get excited . . .*

Zoe doesn't want to sound like a crazy person. Been there, done that, as part of the awfulness of being thirteen. Never again, she's promised herself. She forces her voice into a calmer register. "Sorry," she says. She doesn't exactly sound normal, even to her own ears, but she keeps working at it. "I just mean . . ." One final steadying breath. "There's no need for that. I'm fine. Really. Thank you for your concern." Strangers. Strangers are acting concerned. About her. She doesn't remember that ever happening before. In her experience, strangers are oblivious. Or casually cruel. She's not exactly sure what to make of this new experience, but the feeling is not unpleasant.

Cell Phone Girl still looks a bit scared of her. "OK," she says, and resumes walking. And talking on her cell phone.

Zoe says, "I just . . . twisted my ankle." She tries to force a laugh, but it comes out more of a snort. "Wow, did I go down fast."

The biker guy pats her shoulder.

With his tattoos and his full beard and his chain jewelry, he probably finds *her*, with her ragged blue hair and Guns N' Roses t-shirt, kind of drab and average-looking.

The others who have stopped to see what was going on—now that they've caught a closer look at that blue hair and slightly seedy clothing—no doubt have her pegged as a clumsy street kid who likely fell because she's on drugs or alcohol. *Back on familiar ground*, Zoe thinks.

But not entirely. They don't all dismiss her. The biker guy and the younger of the two fast-food place guys and a woman wearing pants with a pattern that should absolutely not even be legal—except, *maybe*, in Hawaii—are gathering her strewn-about papers for her. Trying to help. With no likely expectation of gain. The Chihuahua just generally gets in everybody's way. Still, the papers are no longer important to Zoe—well, they *are*, but they aren't. In any case, she doesn't have the heart to tell these nice people, "Never mind."

I need to let go, she tells herself. *I need to let go.*

She tries not to let her brain dwell on the last twenty-three minutes—*any* of the last twenty-three minutes. She tries not to remember the way she was startled by the blueness of Daniel's eyes. By the way his fingers brushed against the skin on the back of her hand.

By the way he asked if she was truly all right.

Truly.

I wish . . . she thinks.

But she only knows one wish that comes true, and it just isn't cooperating today. It rarely does, but today it's being dramatically disobliging.

I'm sorry, she thinks to the people in and around the bank, whose names she doesn't even know, who in turn don't know they have fewer than twenty minutes to live. And to the one whose name she does know.

She repeats it out loud, because that's what she's used to doing, since that's the way the playback spell—or ability, or curse—works; it needs to be said out loud. "I'm sorry."

Yeah. A lot of good *sorry* has ever accomplished.

But the woman in the exceptionally awful pants thinks Zoe is talking to her and to the other people chasing down Zoe's papers. She smiles encouragingly and says, "Nothing to apologize for, dear. Everybody needs help sometimes."

Not me, Zoe thinks. *I can take care of myself.* Needy people do not survive the system.

A memory bubbles to the top of Zoe's brain from when she was nine or maybe ten years old: Her mother demanding an apology for something-or-other; herself saying, "Sorry"; her mother smacking her across the mouth hard enough Zoe could taste blood; then her mother saying, "No, you weren't. But I bet you are now."

64

And she was right, Zoe thinks.

There's nothing worse than being sorry after it's too late.

If she doesn't at least try to do something, she knows she'll regret it for the rest of her life.

She also knows the irony of what *the rest of her life* might mean.

But she has enough regrets without this.

She tells herself again: She does not have to go back into the bank. There has to be another way.

"Thank you," she tells the woman with the flamboyantly floral pants, the biker guy, the fast-food place guy. "Thank you. I don't need the papers." She doesn't like abandoning them where these strangers—kind as they've tried to be—can read them. She doesn't like the idea of sharing her life story. But some things are more important than others.

She stands, with Biker Guy looking ready to grab and steady her, should she turn out to be wobbly.

But she's not.

Her knees sting from the fall, but she takes off running, and if any of them thinks she's pretty fast for someone who supposedly twisted her ankle, she's already too far away for them to tell her so.

There's no being sure what time it is, except it isn't raining yet, so that might mean she's not too late.

She turns the corner of the block with Spencerport Savings and Loan and, about halfway between her and the bank, sees Daniel just leaving a huge old Victorian house that's been divided into offices.

She runs even faster, but is never going to catch up. As he puts his hand out to open the door of the bank, she calls, "Daniel!"

Only then does she wonder if he gave her his real name: her, a clumsy, pushy, strange-looking stranger in a bank, who had for no apparent reason demanded personal information. She knows that in similar circumstances she has made things up, as a game, a private joke. If he has done the same, she has lost valuable time.

But apparently he's more trustworthy than she is.

He turns.

And waits for her.

And continues to wait, even when the bank guard opens the door to let a woman customer out and to let Daniel come in. Daniel shakes his head and motions for the guard to go ahead and close the door without him.

Zoe is huffing when she reaches him. "Daniel?" she repeats.

"Yes?" He's wearing his sunglasses, and she can't see his eyes, can't read his expression. But of course he doesn't recognize her: This is the very first time he's ever met her.

She says, "Daniel, I need to talk to you."

He looks a bit bemused as he admits, "I'm sorry—do I know you?"

"I'm Zoe," she says. "We've sort of met. But I never told you my name."

"OK," he says slowly, though she hasn't really offered much of an explanation.

"I need to talk to you," she repeats.

And *he* repeats, "OK," though she strongly suspects he's not pleased. As though to prove this, he finishes, "I have some business in the bank. It should only take a few minutes, and then I can come back out and—"

"No!" she practically shouts at him.

His eyebrows go up.

She really *does* need to practice saying *no* without raising her voice and sounding all borderline-demented.

"Sorry, sorry," she says, her hands fluttering ineffectually as she wonders how she can quickly make him see that she's harmless. "I just mean . . . Please. This is important."

He hesitates, which is better than refusing.

She adds, "This is like life-and-death important," which is true but probably sounds overdone. "Please," she repeats. "Can we go back to where you work?" She angles her head toward the Victorian house. "This won't take very long." Under twenty minutes, but she doesn't want to say so. "And it's about to start raining."

He glances back the way she's looked, then at her. Then he says, "The Fitzhugh House? That's not where I work." Great, so now he knows the only way she could have made that mistake is if she's been watching him. He probably suspects she's a weird teenage stalker.

But then he checks the sky and relents. "Coffee?" he asks, nodding to the Dunkin' Donuts two doors down from the card shop. "Or . . ." —he's obviously considering her age, or lack thereof—"hot chocolate?"

She *knew* he would think of her as a kid.

"Yes, please."

They almost make it across the street before the clouds open up.

"Good call," Daniel says once they're safely indoors. He's taken off the raindrop-splattered sunglasses, and she sees that it wasn't just the light in the bank—his eyes really are that blue.

Still, that's no reason for her to get all giddy.

He orders and pays for two hot chocolates.

Which, she tells herself, does not mean they're on a date. He's still too old for her, and they come from different worlds. She and her friends have been drinking coffee—most of them taking it black—since they were thirteen. When, at fourteen, Zoe had her first beer, she was somewhat of a late starter. Not that she drinks beer regularly: She isn't fond of the taste, and mostly she doesn't like feeling out of control. Life seems out of control enough as it is.

She lets Daniel live in his fantasy that she's young and innocent, and he brings two cups to the table in the corner where he's told her to go ahead and sit. "I didn't think to check if you wanted whipped cream," he apologizes.

"Well, yeah," she says, since as far as she's concerned there's no question: If she's going to drink hot chocolate, it had better have whipped cream. She eats a couple spoonfuls of the cool, sweet topping before stirring the rest into the cocoa.

Daniel waits while she sips at the chocolate, which is too hot to actually drink. When she puts her hands around the cup for warmth, he prompts her, "So we met . . . where?"

"In the bank," Zoe says. Not knowing if he does business with more than the one, she tips her chin to indicate Spencerport Savings and Loan, which they can just see through the doughnut place's steamed-up window, beyond the driving rain.

Daniel nods, but says, "I'm sorry, I don't remember."

"Well, you wouldn't," Zoe tells him.

He takes that the wrong way and apologizes: "I'm usually pretty good with faces."

Ooh, he's just tried to tell her: *No, no, don't say you're unmemorable—even though . . . oops! I guess I've just said you are.*

"This is very difficult," she says.

In a gentle voice he asks, "Has someone hurt you? Or threatened you in some way?"

Yeah, and where is she going to go with that question?

Instead of answering, she says, "What I need to say is going to be difficult for you to believe. I need to tell you something so strange it's scary."

"OK," he says, sounding somewhere between wary and amused. Definitely more on the amused side. She even wonders if he might not be faking the wariness entirely, to pretend he's taking her seriously, in order not to humiliate her thoroughly.

Still, she likes the tendency he has to draw out the word *OK*, as though giving it real thought.

But she is no closer to knowing how to start. She says, "I think I need to circle around and take this from a different direction." Not that she's actually chosen *any* direction.

He tells her, "Take your time."

Definitely a lawyer, she decides, and not a businessman. She suspects he's used to people telling him secrets they wouldn't dare tell anyone else, revealing what they've done, what they fear, baring their hearts—with him listening and not flinching.

Not judging?

She, herself, finds it hard not to judge.

Snap judgments can be a very handy tool for someone who has only herself to count on in a harsh world.

She says, "Something very bad is going to happen. I know this for a fact, and it's how I know it that's . . . where the believability factor comes in."

He nods for her to continue.

"Can you promise me ten minutes?" she asks. "Ten minutes

during which I won't appear to be making sense?"

"Have to," Daniel points out. "Or I'll have bought the hot chocolate for nothing." He's smiling, but she's pretty sure he's taking her seriously.

So far.

Part of the reason she's asked for ten minutes is that the man who will be robbing the bank has just pulled his car up in front of the card shop.

Something about Daniel has set the thief off each time that Zoe has seen. The fact that the man began shooting even when Zoe wasn't there makes her suspect that then, too, Daniel got in the way: trying to prevent the robbery, trying to protect other people, since that seems to be his nature. Perhaps all she needs to do is keep him out of there. Then the robber won't go all ballistic; then nobody has to die. So what if the robber makes off with all the money in the bank? That's acceptable. She even has his license plate number—Highly Deranged Person 347—that she could give to the police.

If only the people in the bank can keep from getting killed.

Zoe absently fiddles with the string on the envelope Daniel has placed on the table between them, and she's *so* pleased with herself for having ditched her own paperwork. If he caught sight of that . . .

She realizes she shouldn't be touching his things, that he might consider this an invasion of his space, even though he's working very hard to keep his face nonjudgmental and friendly, both trusting and trustworthy.

And trust is the issue here.

She is not going to try to bullshit him.

"When I was thirteen," she starts, "something happened. I'm

70

not sure I understand the specifics of exactly *what*, and I definitely don't know *why*. But all of a sudden I found that I could . . ." It's like pulling off a bandage, Zoe tells herself: best to get it over with quickly. "I could . . . revisit . . . a time that I'd already lived through. Sort of. To a limited extent."

She hesitates, trying to gauge his reaction. She can't read him.

He asks, "How do you mean?" Gathering more information before committing to a decision. It strikes her as a very lawyerly thing to do.

It's been a couple years since she tried to explain playback. And that didn't go well. That *spectacularly* didn't go well. Zoe is beginning to think she should probably count this playback as a lost cause and start over. The only thing that holds her back is that she has no idea what she'd do in its place.

If her plan works—if keeping Daniel away from the bank is all that's necessary—then what she says is not really all that important. She just needs to keep him occupied for another ten minutes or so. At the worst, he'll think she's a nutcase. Like that's a new experience for her. It isn't as though she'll ever see him again.

But she isn't sure she can keep him here without telling him what she knows.

And if the plan doesn't work, then she might as well have tried *something*, possibly learned something.

Through the rain and the condensation on the window, she can make out the robber entering the bank. Which means the time is 1:29. She has exactly ten minutes left if she's going to replay this time. But her hope, of course, is that she won't have to. It makes her anxious that the combination of distance and weather prevents her from seeing inside through the bank's large window.

Zoe tells Daniel, "It's sort of like hitting the rewind button for a movie. Things back up for twenty-three minutes . . ." She's making an inane gesture, moving her hand from right to left as though pushing something back, which demonstrates nothing, so she clasps her hands together on the table to force them into stillness. "So the movie restarts from that point and plays itself exactly the same as before . . . just as movies always do . . . except for me. For everybody else, it's like the first time. They have no memory of having lived through it before. Of saying and doing and seeing and hearing everything already. Only I know. Only I can instigate change by what *I* say and do."

Daniel is as good at keeping his face blank as her doctors were.

She really hopes he doesn't turn out to be a doctor.

She remembers the original time, before it became a story line, in the bank, when they first realized the place was getting held up. He saw the robber. There was that flicker of something she still can't quite put her finger on—maybe a presentiment of his own death? Then it was like Daniel closed his emotions down, and his face was saying, *OK, I'm not playing this game anymore.* Absorbing information, not showing anything of what he was thinking.

Of course, they quickly went from there to him getting his head blown off.

She twitches at the memory.

Which she sees Daniel note. He asks, "Why twenty-three minutes?"

"Not a clue," she admits.

He sighs. "Can you give me an example?"

72

She figures a nice instance from somebody else's life will work a lot better than telling Daniel what lies in his future. "When I was thirteen . . ." She stops, thinking, *Yeah, at the beginning of when I was thirteen and life was normal, one minute following another and no going back.* She doesn't say that. She swallows hard and starts over. "When I was thirteen, my friend Jessie and I were riding our bikes on the sidewalk. On our own block. We were racing, which—all right, all right—we shouldn't have been doing." Zoe doesn't want him getting sidetracked, the way Dr. Shaheen did, about unsafe behaviors. Zoe says, "She was ahead of me. And at one point she looked over her shoulder to see how close I was. And just then the Greenbergs were backing up out of their driveway, and she was going down the sidewalk like a bat out of hell, and she didn't see them, and they didn't see her, and she smacked right into their car, right . . . I don't know what that's called . . . behind the back passenger door, kind of where the gas cap is? What is that—the fender?"

He nods, either to acknowledge that it is in fact a fender she's describing, or simply to indicate for her to get on with her story.

"And there was like one heartbeat where I thought, *Hey, at least she wasn't two seconds faster, or she would have been run over.* And then Jessie and the bike went flipping over the trunk of the Greenbergs' car, and she went sliding into the street, right under the wheels of another car. She . . ." It took months before Zoe could get the picture out of her mind, and now here she's gone and invited it back in. "You didn't need to look close to know she was dead."

Zoe has come to realize during the telling of this story that his steely-eyed poker face does not come naturally to him, because he's lost track of watching over what his expression reveals. Which is a good thing, she supposes. Would she be able to trust someone who could hear about Jessie's death *without* wincing?

She continues, "I stopped my bike, and I couldn't believe what had happened, how fast it had happened. You know? Not a hint of danger, of worrying, of thinking, *Maybe racing isn't such a smart idea.* And then that collision. I put my arms around myself . . ." Zoe sees that her hands, apparently possessing a mind of their own, are no longer dutifully on the table where she put them, but are hugging herself. She very carefully clasps her hands in front of herself again, where she can keep an eye on them and not accidentally initiate a playback.

Daniel is watching all this with his I-am-a-rock face once again in place.

She tells him, "And I was wishing I could do it all again. A do-over. Before getting on our bikes, Jessie and I had been playing one of her Nancy Drew video games, and they have this 'Try Again' feature—if you make a mistake and get killed, you can restart from right before you made your bad decision, and go through that section of the game again. And that's what I wanted, and that's what I said out loud. Not because I thought anything would happen, but because I was kind of in shock. Everybody had rushed out of their cars—the driver who'd run over her, Mr. and Mrs. Greenberg, their assorted kids and nephews and nieces—there were always too many Greenbergs to keep track of. They were all . . ." Once again, the exact word she's looking for eludes her. Plus, she realizes she's talking like a thirteen-year-old, as though she's channeling her younger self, and she's unable to stop. "They were all . . . whatever the *frantic* version of milling about is. Yelling, 'Call 911!' Yelling for a doctor, a blanket, Jessie's mom. Nobody sure what to do because there very obviously *wasn't* anything to do. So I said, to nobody in particular, just babbling, I said: 'I wish I could try again. I wish I could play back time . . .' And all of a sudden, Jessie and I were in her garage, with her leaning down to put some air in my tires 'cause they were kind of wonky."

Daniel takes a breath, and she keeps on talking, not giving him a chance for questions. "And I was like 'Whoa!' and she was like 'What?' And that was the first time. Jessie had no memory of any of it. She was all, 'Well, if you don't want to race, just say so. We don't have to race.' And I was all, 'No, but we did: down Thurston, around the corner to Congress, then around the corner to Fairview, and you smacked right into the Greenbergs' car.' And she said, 'It's Saturday—the Greenbergs aren't allowed to leave their house,' and I said, 'Greenbergs don't keep Sabbath if Mrs. Greenberg wants to go out to dinner,' and Jessie still didn't believe me, so we got on our bikes, but we'd spent so much time arguing that we were just going around the first corner when we saw the Greenbergs drive by."

Zoe can tell she's given Daniel way too much background information, but this is the first time in so long that she's talked about that day, the words come spilling out of her as inexorably as Jessie going over the back of the Greenbergs' car.

"OK," Daniel says, trying to process it all. "So . . ."

"So, Jessie kind of believed me, on account of she *saw* the Greenbergs' car. Her mother didn't. Her mother eventually said maybe we shouldn't hang around together so much."

Zoe suspects that right about now Daniel might be identifying with Jessie's mom.

Zoe says, "Did I not warn you that you would find this hard to believe?"

"Fair warning indeed." Daniel starts again, "So . . . you've told other people?"

"Yes."

"And you've done this reliving of an incident other times, too? Besides with Jessie and the Greenbergs?"

"You're missing the point."

He looks relieved to hear this, as though still hoping the conversation might turn rational.

Zoe doubts her further explanation will keep him relieved for long. She checks out the window facing the bank and sees—so far—no sign of commotion. She says, "Let's say that at exactly twenty-three minutes after the hour, something bad happens."

Daniel has seen her eyes flick toward the window, and he, too, glances outside. "Any particular hour?" he asks.

"No."

"Any particular bad thing?"

"No."

"Am I one of the Greenbergs?"

"What? No." She puts her hands on her hips and stares him down. "Why would you even ask that?"

"Don't know," he admits. "People not remembering things. All those Greenbergs unaccounted for . . . I thought you were going to tell me I have amnesia."

Zoe suspects he is trying to break the tension. Either that, or his mind has begun to wander. She says, "You're supposed to be taking this seriously."

"I am," he protests, though he clearly is not. "Sorry," he says, though he clearly is not that, either. "Just checking."

"No amnesia," Zoe says. "No stray Greenbergs. Twenty-three

minutes after *an* hour—the time chosen purely for illustrative purposes and for the sake of saving me from having to do math—something happens that I feel needs changing. I say, 'Playback,' which plays back time, which goes back twenty-three minutes—in this example, just to make a point, to the hour. I try to improve things by doing something differently. But I don't like the way it's going. So, maybe twenty-after, I call it quits. I say, 'Playback' again. Suddenly it's exactly on the hour again—even though I only used part of the twenty-three minutes. I can keep on going back and keep on going back—always to the exact same starting point—until I'm happy. Or, more likely, till I'm willing to settle. Or, up to ten tries. And the other limitation is, once the time goes past twenty-three minutes, then that's it. Once minute number twenty-four starts, that whole previous twenty-three-minute block of time is closed, and I can't go back any more than anybody else can. Oh, yeah, and the last limitation is: I can't take anybody or anything with me. Which means nobody else remembers. So it's kind of hard to prove."

"I can imagine," Daniel says. Then, seeing her don't-talk-down-to-me look, adds, "The hard-to-prove bit."

"Uh-huh," Zoe says. She watches him taking all this in, then adds, "I'm not on any prescription meds."

He asks, "Are you *supposed to be* on any prescription meds?"

"Not at the moment. I gave up trying to convince people. It was just easier that way. So, no more meds, and visits with a psychiatrist only once a month."

"And you're telling me this . . . ?"

"Because something bad has happened. Something very, very bad. I've been trying to change it."

Daniel, clever young man that he is, catches on. "Which is

where—or, rather, *when*—we met before? How you learned my name?"

But even though he's said it, she suspects he doesn't believe it.

"We both know that my knowing your name does not prove we've met. All sorts of ways I could have learned *that*. So what I'd like you to do is come up with a secret word or phrase that has meaning only to you." She can tell he's not following. Before he can ask, she says, "I don't mean your computer password or social security number." The last thing she needs is for him to suspect she's trying a scam. "And I don't mean something you make up here and now. Maybe something from your past. Something that—next time I see you—when I say it, you'll know there's no way I could be familiar with that word or phrase or idea except by your telling me." She sighs. "You don't understand."

"No kidding," he tells her.

"It's not that I'm asking you to give me a word that will help you remember me. I'm asking for a word that only has meaning to you, so if a stranger comes up to you and says that word, you'd . . ." She drifts off, thinking the whole thing is hopeless.

"The stranger being you?"

She nods, but he sits back in his chair and she can tell he's done humoring her.

"One more minute," she says. "I'm not asking you to tell me right now."

"Zoe . . ." Daniel shakes his head. "I wish I could help you, I really do—"

"There's a man across the street, even now, as we speak," Zoe says all in a rush, "robbing the bank."

That's gotten him focused again.

He's looking out the window, although he can't make out what's going on inside the bank any more than she could.

Outside the bank, however, Zoe sees that this time, finally, the woman with the stroller has reached her car, parked in front of the bank. She has turned on the engine to warm the car, and has gotten her child unstrapped from the stroller. She is now half-in/half-out of the backseat of the car as she works to fasten the toddler into his car seat, while the stroller—and her lower half—continues to get rained on.

It must be almost 1:39. *Then* it won't be up to Zoe anymore.

"I don't know the man," she assures Daniel. "It's not that I overheard plans or anything like that. But I was in the bank the first time it happened. And so were you."

Daniel stands up, as though he feels compelled to be doing something but has no idea what that should be.

"What time is it?" Zoe asks.

Daniel looks surprised she needs to ask—as though everyone in the world has a cell phone—but he checks his. "One thirty-seven. When you say—"

Zoe interrupts, knowing she only has about a minute and a half before this twenty-three minutes will close to her. "Never mind," she says.

Let Daniel think she's a grade-A crazy. The robber has not shot anyone, and she is going to assume he will not. Of course, someone could get killed at minute twenty-four, and then everybody will be out of luck.

But this is not her problem.

"*Never mind?*" Daniel echoes, somewhere between incredulous and angry.

"I think it's fixed itself," Zoe tells him. She watches the young mother back out of her car.

The door to the bank flies open.

No no no! Zoe thinks, figuring the robber has picked the worst possible moment to make his getaway from the bank.

But it isn't the robber. It's one of the customers who comes running out.

There's the crack of a gunshot, and the customer goes sprawling on the sidewalk.

More shots.

Screams heard through the open doorway.

Now the robber *does* run out. He collides with the young mother. He shoots her, then jumps into her car, probably not yet even noticing the child in the backseat. Not yet. He takes off with a squeal of tires.

Daniel's eyes have gotten big. He is looking at her in horror, as though she's the one responsible for all this.

Which she is.

In a way.

Staff and customers from Dunkin' Donuts crowd around the window to see what is going on, blocking Zoe and Daniel's view.

He asks her, "It happens like this every time?"

"There are differences," she says.

She suspects he knows what one of those differences might be. But he says, "If you can change things, you have to try again."

So she comes out and says it: "I've seen you die."

She sees him take in this information. Mentally weigh things. He considers. He may even try to talk sense into himself. But, if so, he fails. He takes a deep breath and says, "Armadillo."

"What?" she asks.

"When you see me next time, tell me that I told you to say *armadillo*."

She nods.

She, too, hesitates.

But in the end she hugs herself. And she says, "Playback."

CHAPTER 8

TIME RESETS TO 1:16.

The situation is not as hopeless as it has seemed. Daniel has become more than a victim, a potential fatality who needs rescuing. He may well be an ally.

Zoe sees a garbage can in front of the store two doors down from Tops 'n Totes. She tosses her formerly precious folder of papers into it as she takes off running toward Independence Street.

Daniel denied working at the converted-into-offices Victorian place, the Fitzhugh House apparently, but she knows she saw him coming out of there. She bursts into the front hall and is faced with a sign listing the people who have offices: one law firm takes up the entire third floor; an evidently smaller law firm and a photographer share the second floor; and the ground floor is home to a real estate agent (Room 1A), an acupuncturist (1B), and someone (1C) described as "M. Van Der Meer, Designer," though designer of *what* the sign doesn't specify.

Zoe takes a second to pull her ponytail out of its elastic. She gives her blue hair a quick fluff-up, telling herself this is to look older and—by extension—more credible. Also, she suspects it's more becoming. *Pathetic*, she chides herself.

A door on the second floor opens, and Zoe hears Daniel's voice, saying thanks and good-bye to someone.

She runs to the staircase with its old-fashioned wooden banister in time to see him close the door labeled 2A, the office of Nicholas Wyand, Attorney-at-Law.

Racing up the stairs, she intercepts him on the landing between the first floor and the second, by the leaded glass window that is letting in the last of the sunshine before the rain will take over.

Daniel has already stepped aside to let her pass, his envelope of papers in one hand, sunglasses in the other.

"Daniel!" she says.

"Yes," he answers, his voice bright to match the enthusiasm of hers, though he makes no attempt to bluff that he has any idea who she is.

"Armadillo," she tells him.

"Excuse me?" he says.

Well, of course she knew it wasn't going to be *that* simple.

ZOE: Daniel!
DANIEL: Yes.
ZOE: Armadillo.
DANIEL: Wow, you must be someone I met and trusted
   in an alternate reality. Tell me what you want me to do.

In place of that scenario, Zoe says, "My name is Zoe. We've never met—well, we have, but not exactly—but you said I should say *armadillo*."

Daniel already looks like he's having trouble keeping up. "I did?"

"It's . . . sort of a code," Zoe explains. She should have asked for more details, but had been too afraid of getting stranded on the wrong side of her allotted twenty-three minutes. Now she has to admit, "I'm . . . not sure what's the significance of the word itself.

83

But my saying it is supposed to let you know you can trust me."

He's amused and intrigued—an expression that very much suits his features.

Zoe hopes she isn't looking at him in the drool-y sort of way she and Rasheena have caught Mrs. Davies looking at actors in those old black-and-white movies from the forties and fifties. Zoe remembers Mrs. Davies sitting in front of the TV. Rasheena asking her, "You like that guy?" Mrs. Davies nodding. Rasheena saying, "Don't you know that guy been dead longer than we been alive?"

Dead guys is not a topic on which Zoe wants her mind dwelling.

So it's a good thing when Daniel says, "I see. Well . . ." He looks around, but there are no chairs in the small lobby, so he sits on the floor of the landing, his feet on the next step going down. Apparently willing to trust her at least long enough to chat with her.

"That's not your office up there?" she asks, just to make sure, in case Daniel was being evasive before because she was coming off as stalkerish. An office would be more comfortable, more private.

"Just visiting someone." The way he chooses that moment to set down the envelope he's been carrying, putting it behind him on the landing, suggests to Zoe that he was seeing the lawyer on the second floor about those papers—which still doesn't mean *he* isn't a lawyer, too. He asks, "You know about *armadillo*, but not where I work?"

He's left room for Zoe to sit next to him, and she does.

It's a bit of a tight fit. She squashes herself against the banister so as not to press against him, and she tells herself not to get flustered by his eyes. Or his hair. Or his smile.

"No," she admits. "Why *armadillo*?"

He hesitates, and she's about to tell him *never mind* when he

84

says, "When I was . . . maybe ten, and I'd been spooked by stories of kids being snatched by strangers who claimed to be sent by parents—that was the code word I told my family to use: *If they absolutely had to send a stranger to pick me up from school or wherever, make sure the stranger said* armadillo, *so I would know they had really sent him.*"

Zoe suspects Daniel's parents were not the kind of people who ever sent strangers to pick up their son from anywhere. Zoe often had strangers pick her up—though more often didn't have *anyone* show when she needed fetching—and yet she never even thought of having a code word. She can't imagine her mother having the patience.

"Why *armadillo?*" Zoe asks. "Are you originally from Texas?" Not that she would have ever thought so from his speech.

"No, I've always lived here," Daniel tells her—which is what she would have guessed. "I suppose it takes someone from Rochester, New York, to think an armadillo is cute."

"OK," Zoe says in the same deliberate manner she's heard him use—just, not yet.

Daniel asks, "So . . . how did we meet—but not exactly—and why did you and I need a code word?"

The whole purpose of having a code word was to get things moving faster, so Zoe jumps right in. She says, "I had just told you something that—on the face of it—seemed impossible. But something happened that made you believe me. That's when you gave me the word."

He's watching her, not closed-faced as when they'd sat in Dunkin' Donuts, but trying to take this all in.

He says slowly, piecing it together, "So you and I have met . . .

and it's not that you've changed your appearance . . . ?"—she shakes her head—"but I don't remember meeting you . . . and you knew I wouldn't remember you . . ." His blue eyes are scrutinizing her, which is disconcerting. He doesn't sound challenging, just looking for information, when he asks, "Why don't I?"

It's to avoid the intensity of his eyes that she glances away from them, from his face. Sitting has caused his jacket to gap, and a glint beneath the jacket catches her attention.

Zoe freezes.

He has a gun.

Damn. *He has a gun.*

Her thoughts ricochet around in her head. He can't be a police officer. He never identified himself as one. And surely he would have. Maybe not that first time in the bank. Conceivably he might have thought that would have just complicated things, with the robber already all freaked out at the bank guard. But surely this last time, when they were talking in the doughnut shop. He would have said, once he believed her: "Zoe, I'm a policeman. I can handle this."

But he didn't.

Who else carries a gun?

Well, her mother did that one time, but Zoe doesn't want to think about that.

Yeah, right. A lot of good *not wanting* does. The thoughts come anyway . . .

The impossibly long ride to the Family Counseling Center, with her parents bickering and sniping all the way, her attempts at making peace only seeming to escalate their hostility playback through playback, her father, who simply would not stop shouting, even once they got into the office. Her mother, finally quiet, pulling the gun from her purse. The family counselor (who would have guessed such a fat old man could move so fast?) diving for cover behind the couch. And she herself too stunned to move, despite the clear hints anybody with any sense would have picked up on. Continuing to sit like a pathetic, useless lump. Like a target, if that had been her mother's intent. Like her mother's accomplice, for all the help she was to Dad.

And there's Delia's ex-boyfriend, the one before the one at the bus stop, the reputed drug dealer. Zoe had given him the benefit of the doubt, not believing what the other girls said about him because she'd thought he looked—well, not exactly upstanding, but not exactly disreputable either. Until that time, watching a pick-up basketball game, he'd pulled out a gun and took a shot at a guy for hogging the ball. Never mind that he'd hit the nearby Dumpster instead of the player, or that he claimed the Dumpster had been his target all along: Zoe has clearly demonstrated she is not good at reading people.

But still. In Zoe's experience, people who have guns fire them.

Who brings a gun to a family counseling session?

Or to a basketball game in a city park?

Who brings a gun to a bank?

Zoe's mind refuses to accept the obvious.

Till suddenly things fall into place.

Daniel can't be trusted. Any more than her mother. Or Delia's ex-boyfriend.

That look? That expression that flitted across Daniel's face when he first saw the bank robber, that emotion or feeling she wasn't able to give a name to? She has a name for it now. That was recognition. Daniel recognized the robber. And now Zoe realizes: The robber recognized Daniel. *That* was why the man started shooting. He knew Daniel could identify him. *That* was why he wanted to take Daniel hostage, and why Daniel balked, why he was so sure he would never survive should he be taken away from witnesses. *He's never going to let me go*, Zoe remembers him saying. *He's never going to let any of us go. So you might as well just shoot him now.*

They recognized each other.

And yet Daniel isn't a cop.

But he's carrying a gun

She had called him *Mr. President* after William Henry Harrison, bad luck president extraordinaire.

How much more bad luck can you have than to be inside a bank, planning to rob it—at the exact same time another robber of your acquaintance walks in to hold up that same bank?

If there are other reasons for Daniel to be carrying a concealed weapon, another explanation for why he recognized the robber, Zoe doesn't have time to try to figure them out.

"Crap!" she says.

She tries to scramble to her feet. But her position is awkward, what with sitting on that step so her knees are higher than her waist, and what with being more or less wedged between Daniel and the banister. Somehow her legs get tangled in his and she teeters on the edge of that top stair.

And all the while, she's still saying, "Crap crap crap!" knowing she's about to fall the entire length of the staircase.

Except that Daniel has caught hold of her wrist. This keeps her from tumbling backward, but also keeps her from being able to transport herself with the playback spell.

"What is it?" he asks. "What's wrong?"

She just barely manages to keep from falling fully onto him by twisting so that—almost as bad—she lands back exactly where she started from, sitting hard, her thigh brushing against his, which, just a few heartbeats ago, would have caused her distress for an entirely different reason.

"Zoe?" he says. Calmly. Gently. Concerned. "What's happened? What's frightened you?"

"Let go of me!" she shouts at him. Once more she tries to stand, tries to yank her arm out of his grasp. Uses her other hand to beat at his hand holding her. "Let go of me!"

Still looking at her with that mixture of confusion and . . . and something that certainly *looks like* the desire to help—he tells her, "Careful. I'm letting go." And then—once he's sure releasing her won't catapult her backward down the stairs—he does: He lets go of her arm.

But he can't be trusted.

She manages to step back onto the less precarious footing of the landing. Away from his touch.

"Zoe," he says, sounding as reasonable as she could have ever wished for, "Don't be afraid. Whatever kind of trouble you're in, let me help you."

But he's the trouble.

She puts her arms around herself and wishes herself away from him.

CHAPTER 9

TIME RESETS TO 1:16.

Zoe's ponytail elastic is once again holding her hair. She is embarrassed for herself—and furious with herself—that she wanted to look nice for Daniel.

She has never felt so betrayed. Not when her mother would hit her. Not when her father would pretend he didn't notice. Not when her friends and her friends' parents and her teachers and her doctors refused to believe her about her ability to play back time.

But this is worse.

All this while she was feeling sorry for him, trying to help him, trying to save him—*risking her life to save him*—and here he is, just as bad as the man who shot him.

Because Daniel, too, brought a gun into the bank. Maybe just to threaten. But surely someone who plans a crime and supplies himself with a weapon knows there's a chance he might end up using it. Some of the kids in the places she's stayed have scars that can prove this. As does her father.

Is it purest coincidence that Zoe has seen Daniel killed? Couldn't it just as easily have ended the exact opposite way?—with Daniel waving the gun and menacing tellers and customers alike, with Daniel shooting the other bank robber point-blank in the head?

Zoe needs some physical release for her anger. Anger management has never been one of her particular problems. But she's heard enough from the other girls to be familiar with some of the buzzwords. A *time-out* doesn't seem relevant for this situation. *Deep breaths. Think before you speak. Identify possible solutions.* She guesses these techniques are as meaningless to the people they're inflicted on as her own doctors' therapies were for her.

She wants to hit someone. Specifically, she wants to hit Daniel, but he's back at the Victorian house, talking to the lawyer on the second floor. Perhaps asking about the legal ramifications of armed robbery. Daniel is a careful person, she thinks (with—all right! all right!—maybe a bit of bitterness): He's a planner. He would surely weigh the consequences and decide if the risks were worthwhile.

How could you? she mentally screams at him.

Some of the boys with whom Zoe has come up through the ranks go to the gym, take out their frustrations on a punching bag. She isn't sure if the girls do this also.

But in any case, Zoe isn't in a gym. She's out on the street, in front of the hat and purse boutique, and there is nothing around that offers itself up as suitable punching material. The brick wall? The window? Zoe isn't so far gone into rage as to injure herself. Or one of the passersby.

Besides, her hands are full. She once more is holding the folder of papers she stole from the group home.

Well, they will have to do.

She will rip the whole folder in half. She's seen people rip a phone book in half, which looks eminently satisfying, and the folder is a fraction of that thickness.

But she finds she isn't strong enough.

She lets the folder itself drop to the street, thinking the manila is too thick. But apparently there are still too many pages. She sticks half under her arm, and still has no luck. Halves what she has left. Still no joy. Half again, and she's barely able to manage that.

This is my life, Zoe thinks, for what the folder holds is the information the group home has gathered on her. All the various doctors' evaluations, the social workers' reports, the P-34 forms filled in by a succession of housemothers.

Except it's not her life. It's people's perceptions of who she is. And they're as wrong about her as she was about Daniel. Destroying this folder full of misinformation in increments of fewer than a dozen pages at a time is not nearly as satisfying as doing the whole thing at once. Or as punching Daniel.

Someone passing by gives a loud *Hmph!* full of scorn and self-satisfaction, and Zoe looks up to see the mother with two children. She isn't sure if it's the mother or the boy who has vocalized this disapproval, but it's the girl who whines, "Mommy, she's littering! She shouldn't be littering! Somebody's going to need to clean up after her!"

"Somebody will," Mommy assures her, hustling both children away.

Coming from the other direction, Miss Aloha-Pants, who once helped Zoe pick up these papers, now aligns herself with the mother and kids, muttering to them while inclining her head to indicate Zoe, "Some people."

Zoe sees that several of the sheets she'd shoved under her arm have slid loose and fallen. *Like there's nothing in the world worse than a litterbug*, Zoe thinks. Still, she stoops to gather them up. And as she does so, drops some of the ragged pieces from the little bit she *was* able to rip.

Her mind flashes back—not a playback, just a vivid memory such as a normal person might have—to being inside the bank with all those deposit and withdrawal slips. Daniel stooping down to help her gather them up. Daniel supplying her with the name that had evaded her recall: Blitzen.

What kind of bank robber, Zoe asks herself, *knows the names of Santa's reindeer?*

Yeah, she retorts to herself, *you wouldn't be so eager to fit a different meaning to what you KNOW was going on if he didn't have those gorgeous blue eyes.*

That's the trouble with the world vs. TV and movies, she reasons. Hollywood makes you think all bad guys *look* like bad guys. Swarthy. Ugly. Yellow-toothed and pockmarked. The kind of guys who kick kittens and spit when they talk.

Not the kind of guys who smile kindly and try to put you at your ease when you've been clumsy and are clearly out of your element. Who try to get overbearing bank guards not to hassle you.

That just goes to prove he has a disregard for authority, Zoe tells herself.

But she knows this is the stupidest thing she's told herself all day.

There's a world of difference between angling to let the bank guard leave her alone so she can be out of the rain, and holding up the bank.

But that's what he was going to do, she reminds herself. He was going to rob the bank.

She tries to convince herself that Daniel is not the kind of bank robber who would start shooting indiscriminately.

But the truth is: She obviously knows nothing about him.

She can't help remembering the first shooting she ever witnessed, which—until today—she had assumed would be the only shooting she ever witnessed: how she sat, paralyzed by shock and fear, while the Family Counseling receptionist—*the receptionist!*—talked Mom into putting the gun down. While the receptionist called for an ambulance. While the receptionist administered the first aid that saved Dad's life. While the receptionist *made excuses for Zoe,* saying, "You're just a kid. You're just thirteen. Of course there was nothing you could do." Letting Zoe off too easily because *she* didn't know about playback. Didn't know Zoe *could have* stopped it, could have made it go away—if only Zoe hadn't squandered her ten playbacks for that particular twenty-three-minute block of time by trying to get Mom and Dad to stop arguing during the ride and in the waiting room.

Proof, finally, of what her mother had always claimed: that Zoe was a waste of time and effort.

If Zoe does nothing this time, the outcome will be the same as when she watched from the card shop. She will not be there to distract Daniel, and somehow or other that results in a whole bunch of people dying.

She realizes where this train of thought is leading because she has skirted this issue already. That the original events were the best: where only Daniel dies—well, and the robber himself—and where she ends up spattered by their blood. Except now she knows Daniel deserves to die.

Sort of.

Well, not really.

She can't convince herself of that.

And no matter if he does deserve it: She can't bring herself to intentionally cause it to happen.

Not because of the eyes, the hair, the smile, the kindness.

But because she's the kind of person who can't make those village-vs.-the-child decisions.

Not deciding is deciding, the sociology teacher had insisted.

Zoe revisits the question she asked herself before: *What kind of bank robber knows the names of Santa's reindeer?*

The question she realizes she *should* be asking herself is: *What kind of bank robber lets himself get distracted by helping an awkward girl feel at ease?*

Daniel has not acted like a bank robber.

But neither has he acted like a policeman. Even an off-duty policeman. Or an FBI agent, for that matter.

Or at least she doesn't think so, with her admittedly limited experience with law enforcement people.

He knew the bank robber, she reminds herself.

Can she let him die? Him, and a whole bunch of others, just because she *thinks* a policeman would have identified himself to her while they were sitting there drinking cocoa and chatting at Dunkin' Donuts?

There wasn't that much time, she tells herself.

First, he didn't know what she wanted.

Then, she sounded like a crazy person, talking about dead friends no longer being dead, and about knowing what was going to happen in the future.

Until what she was saying started to happen. Until he saw for himself. And only then was he convinced. Or maybe he just wanted to believe because he couldn't stand watching those people in the bank get killed. Even after she warned him, *I've seen you die*, he gave her the word *armadillo*.

Rather than saying, "I'm a policeman."

Which might have seemed irrelevant at the time.

She mutters to herself, "Blitzen."

The biker guy walking his Chihuahua glances her way with a sour expression and asks, "You talking to me?" in a tone that indicates she'd better not be.

Zoe ignores him. She puts her arms around herself and says, "Playback."

CHAPTER 10

T IME RESETS TO 1:16.

Zoe doesn't take the ten seconds to tuck her folder under her shirt or the five extra steps to dump it into the trash. She just clutches the pack of papers, but doesn't worry if she loses bits and pieces of it—the story of her former life—as she runs as fast as she can to Independence Street. To the Fitzhugh House. She slams the front door so hard that a man—possibly the M. Van Der Meer of "M. Van Der Meer, Designer"—opens his first-floor door to peek out at her.

She scowls, not even exactly in his direction, and he retreats back into his room.

A moment later, she hears Daniel's voice as he takes leave of the second-floor office.

Zoe has remained by the foot of the stairs, safe from Daniel's touch. Safe from the blueness of his eyes.

He's about to start down the stairs when she calls up to him, "Are you a policeman?"

Daniel ponders her, or the question, a moment before answering, "No . . ."

Zoe considers turning and leaving.

Instead, she says, "But you're carrying a gun."

Daniel glances around the foyer. Perhaps he doesn't like her broadcasting this information. Perhaps he's being alert for ambush, which either a policeman or a bank robber might be. Even more slowly than he gave his previous answer, he says, "Yes . . ."

Every nerve ending is telling Zoe to get out of there.

She's getting pretty good at ignoring her instincts.

But she does have her arms wrapped around herself, ready. She can say *playback* faster than he can get downstairs. Faster, she hopes, than he can draw the gun, if that becomes his intent. Though it's hard to think of him doing that. She asks, "Are you planning on robbing the bank?"

Like ANYONE would answer yes, Zoe chides herself.

His expression says he's surprised by her question, incredulous that she would ask, and that he's wondering who the hell she is.

Instead of sharing any of that, he tells her, "No, to the bank question. Let me show you something. Don't be alarmed." He's started down the stairs again, while simultaneously reaching into the inside pocket of his jacket.

And as soon as he's said not to be alarmed, Zoe is more alarmed than ever.

"Don't come any closer," she warns, stepping backward, toward the door.

Daniel stops partway down. He's holding a card, which he tosses in her direction.

Of course, Zoe is totally distracted by trying to catch it—and yet still manages to miss. But fortunately Daniel doesn't take advantage, and stays where he is even while she goes to pick it up off the floor.

The card is laminated, and there's a picture of Daniel. For a moment Zoe thinks he's showing her his driver's license. Then the words sink in:

Daniel Lentini

Private Investigator

"OK?" he asks. "May I come down? You're not afraid of me?"

She looks up at him and doesn't know what to say.

Private investigator. It was not a possibility that had even crossed her mind.

I almost let him die, Zoe thinks. *I assumed the worst, and I was prepared to let him die.*

He takes her silence as permission to move.

She's aware of him walking down the stairs slowly, evidently to avoid spooking her—either that, or for dramatic effect—and she has yet to make up her mind if this is a good thing or bad.

She still hasn't decided, even when he's standing directly in front of her.

He's not exactly annoyed, but neither is he amused. He says, "And now it's my turn: Who are you? What's going on?"

ANYBODY can have a card printed, she tells herself. She also tells herself that if she hadn't changed her mind, he would have died, and it would have been on her soul.

She says, "I—I saw the gun, and I . . ." The identification card has started vibrating.

Oh.

No, it hasn't: It's Zoe's hand that is shaking. "I thought . . . I thought . . ."

Somehow or other that image has come back into her head: Daniel, his eyes wide and blue and frightened and defiant, saying "Take the shot," and the guard taking the shot. The guns going off, near simultaneously. The feeling of Daniel's blood hitting her skin.

He recognized the robber; the robber recognized him. And Daniel didn't say out loud what he knew, so that the robber wouldn't be provoked into killing anybody else.

He died then to protect them, and now she almost let him get killed yet again.

Her knees are about to buckle, and she puts her hand out to grab the banister. Either she misses entirely, or Daniel intercepts her, but in any case he takes her by the arm, telling her, "Sit."

She sits, on the bottom step.

And suddenly Zoe is shaking so hard she can't stop.

Ditto for Zoe crying.

She almost let him die.

She is less than worthless.

The door of 1C, the Designer, cracks open, and Zoe screams, "Go away!"

The door snaps shut.

Daniel sits down next to her and instinctively goes to put a comforting arm around her. Then clearly thinks better of that idea. Being in the system, Zoe has heard social workers talk about the conundrum. Adult guys who have *any* possibility of *ever* even *potentially* working with children—priests, teachers, caseworkers, police—Zoe knows they've all had it drummed into their heads: Under no circumstances are they to touch a minor unless it's to actually pick them up off the floor if they've fallen, or out of the pool if they're drowning, or away from a building that's burning.

And, even then—witnesses preferred.

But Zoe can't stop crying, and Daniel reconsiders again. He puts both arms around her and holds her, self-consciously but gently.

She buries her face in his chest and sobs. He'll never be able to get all the tears and snot and drool out of his jacket, she tells herself.

He doesn't say a word—which is good. He knows he doesn't know what the situation is, so how can he assure her that everything is going to be all right? He just rocks her, very, very gently, and holds her.

Ridiculous as such a feeling is, Zoe has never felt safer in her life. And that *is* ridiculous. Daniel is right up there with President-for-only-thirty-two-days William Henry Harrison as a lightning rod for disaster. Who, with any sense at all, holds onto a lightning rod?

Eventually Zoe gains enough control to be mortified, to wish there were a restroom nearby that she could duck into so she could stick her face under some cold water. Like for maybe a day or two. Of course, to a certain extent, she could do this, but initiating a playback at this point seems a bit irrelevant, unless you count saving yourself from humiliation as relevant.

Daniel hands her a linen hankie and stands up to give her room to pull herself together.

She wipes her eyes first, then mops up the rest of her face. Now what? She has never had a guy—or anyone, for that matter—hand her anything more substantial than a disposable tissue. Is she supposed to return the hankie to him, all damp and nasty as it is, or consider it a gift? In the best of all possible worlds, she supposes she should launder it and return it at a later date.

But this is obviously not the best of all possible worlds.

She looks for him and finds him by the door, picking up her papers, which are strewn about the entryway. She has apparently once again dropped her folder—this time without even noticing when it left her hands.

He is unapologetically reading the papers.

And this time there are no lists of reindeer names.

Daniel comes and sits down next to her again. The top page is the intake form from when she moved into the first group home, the one on Alexander Street. It's the part of the psych evaluation where Dr. Shaheen describes how Zoe is delusional, believing she can travel through time and space at will, making it sound all Syfy-channel stupid.

She tells Daniel, "The one on the green sheet is far less unsettling." Even though, really, Daniel looks more interested than unsettled.

He sorts through the pages till he finds the transcript of her conversation with Dr. Shaheen where Zoe admits she made up the time travel stuff in order to get attention when her parents were getting divorced. Daniel says, "I'm not sure he sounds entirely convinced."

Zoe says, "As well he shouldn't have been. The divorce came about *because* of me, because of my perceived mental health issues. All he needed to do was check the dates."

Daniel asks, "So you're retracting your retraction?"

"Yes," she admits.

"And . . . you brought these papers to me . . . why?"

"Actually I didn't," Zoe says. "I dropped them accidentally. My group home is shifting to a paperless office, so they're in the process

102

of uploading all of this stuff onto their computer. Once they're done, the paper files will be shredded. I'm not the techie sort who can hack into computer systems. But anyone with a paper clip could pick the cheap little lock on the office door. I just wanted to see what they were saying about me. Decide for myself what I wanted to leave to be scanned into the computer. I really kind of specifically *didn't* want you to see."

"Oops," Daniel says.

Zoe says, "They kind of make a bad first impression."

Daniel gives a noncommittal grunt. Then adds, "Sort of like carrying a gun might do."

"Hmm," Zoe says. He doesn't seem overly concerned by the fact that she's been under psychiatric care, so she's emboldened to ask, "So what do *your* papers say?"

He glances at the envelope which he's left unguarded on the step behind her. But she's been too busy making a spectacle of herself to snoop. "Just trust fund stuff."

Ooh, trust fund. Zoe's heard of trust funds. If she understands the concept correctly, they're for people who have more money than they know what to do with—money, and irresponsible kids who can't be relied on not to run through the family fortune faster than it's made. She *knew* Daniel was out of her class, no matter what their ages.

He asks her, "Where, exactly, did you see me when I frightened you?"

"Here," Zoe says. "About ten minutes ago. Or in about ten minutes. Depending on how you look at it."

"Oh." Daniel refuses to rise to the bait, to become visibly troubled at her words.

"I was supposed to tell you *armadillo*."

"Were you?" he asks. "Told by whom?"

Zoe is charmed by his correct usage of *whom*. Rasheena has called her OCD about grammar. Zoe tells him, "Told by you."

"The last time we met," he finishes for her, "ten minutes . . . one way or the other."

"Actually," she says, "it was the time before the last."

"I see."

"As a code, or password," she explains. "A shortcut. So you'd believe this . . . rather unbelievable story I'm telling you."

He puts out his hand for her to give him back his ID card.

She looks at it one last time, then with uncanny precision of mind, she zeroes in on the single absolutely most irrelevant factor of the entire day. She says, "Lentini? You're Italian?"

With his light brown hair and blue eyes, he looks close to the opposite of Italian, but he only shrugs as he puts the card away.

"So you're a private eye?" Zoe thinks of Mrs. Davies and the old-time black-and-white movies she likes to watch. "Like Sam Spade in *The Maltese Falcon*?"

"Shit, no," Daniel says with a sudden laugh, then immediately catches himself and hurriedly repeats a simple "No," apparently in consideration of her young and presumably delicate ears. He says, "So you knew about *armadillo*, but not that I'm a private investigator?"

She nods.

"OK. And why are we here?"

Before answering, she asks him, "Can you keep track of the time? I absolutely need to leave by 1:38."

His eyebrows go up, but he doesn't ask her to clarify what,

exactly, she means by *leave*. He takes out his cell phone and sets it on top of her folder. "No phone of your own?" he asks.

"No." She sees that the time is 1:29. Now, she realizes that she's been hearing for a few minutes the sound of rain hitting the front door and the window on the landing, though she hadn't really noticed when it started.

Nine minutes. How could she have let this playback get so out of control? There isn't enough time left to try to intervene at the bank. She must use these nine minutes to learn what she can, including how to convince Daniel about what is going on.

She says, "I really can travel back in time, but only to revisit the last twenty-three minutes. Nobody else realizes they've already lived through those twenty-three minutes. Only me. So people keep on doing and saying exactly what they did the first time, unless something *I* do or say causes them to react differently. And what I'm doing differently *this* time is explaining to you, planning with you. So that I'll be better prepared for next time, knowing what to say, and what works, and what's a waste of time."

"OK . . .," he says in the careful way she finds so appealing, not exactly buying into her story wholeheartedly, but not dismissing it either.

"The reason I've traveled back is because I saw the bank get robbed. You were there, too."

"And you thought I was involved?"

"Not the first time, but . . . yeah, later on I came to doubt you."

Daniel asks, "You can do this time travel thing over and over?"

The phone's display shifts to 1:30.

"Not indefinitely," Zoe admits. "Ten playbacks is it."

"And which playback are we currently in?"

Zoe counts up.

Stopping the woman with the two kids and borrowing the phone to call the police . . .

Trying to alert the bank guard, then watching from the card shop . . .

Returning to the bank and getting shot . . .

Sidetracking Daniel into Dunkin' Donuts . . .

Seeing Daniel's gun and going all freakazoid about it . . .

Coming to realize she couldn't just let him get killed but that too much time had passed to intercept him . . .

Here and now. Where, again, she's squandered valuable time.

"Oh crap." It's more often than she had realized. Dangerously more often. How could she have been so careless? "This is the seventh playback."

"OK," Daniel says. "So why, exactly, do you keep going back?"

"Because I keep trying, but I can't fix it so nobody gets hurt. Because that first time, the robber shot you."

"*Shot?*" he repeats.

"Killed," she clarifies.

He's still not one hundred percent with her, but he's believing the *possibility* of what she's saying enough to look at least somewhat apprehensive. Not panicked, but cautious. She supposes it's pretty hard to be cavalier about someone—even someone with the papers to prove she's officially been diagnosed as crazy—foretelling your death.

1:31.

Zoe says, "I went back in time, tried calling the police. Even more people got killed. Got you not to go in. Still, he ended up shooting a bunch of people. Nothing I've tried worked."

106

"Why did you think having me not be there would keep him from shooting?"

"Because you recognized him," Zoe explains.

"So who is he?"

Exasperated, Zoe says, "You didn't say."

"That was pretty unaccommodating of me."

She worries he's veering into skepticism again, but then he asks, "Well, what did he look like?"

Zoe wishes people wouldn't keep asking her that. "Hard to say. White guy. Older than you." She's suddenly sidetracked. "By the way, how old *are* you?" Not that it really makes any difference, but it would be nice if he turned out to be younger than he looks.

"Twenty-five," Daniel answers. Then changes that to, "Well . . . I will be. Soon."

She guesses that he rounds his age up to give himself more credibility as a private investigator, to imply more experience. Still. Twenty-four, or almost twenty-five. "Yeah," Zoe says. "Twenty-five. Me, too. Soon."

Daniel flashes her a quick smile which makes her willing to forgive the almost-ten-year difference in their ages. Though, of course, there's no way he would feel the same.

1:32.

Zoe says, "So I'm guessing he was closer to . . . I don't know . . . forty, maybe. I noticed he was a bit shorter than you." She indicates up to about the top of Daniel's nose. "I couldn't see his hair because he was wearing a Red Wings cap."

"Ah!" Daniel says. "A Red Wings fan."

"Does that mean something to you?" Zoe asks, relieved at how easy this has turned out to be.

"No," Daniel says. "Eyes?"

Zoe tries to remember. "Yes," she finally declares definitively. "Two."

Daniel sighs. "Could you at least see his eyebrows? What color were they?"

Zoe considers. "Dark."

Daniel asks, "So, probably brown eyes?"

She didn't notice them the first time, but forces herself to picture when he aimed his gun at her. She flinches, then nods. "Yeah."

Daniel notices, but doesn't comment on, the flinch. "Beard?" he asks. "Scars? Birthmark? Tattoos? Gold teeth? One leg shorter than the other? Name tag, or place of employment embroidered on his shirt?"

Zoe has been shaking her head. Now she says, "I think you're beginning to get off track."

"Accent?"

She shakes her head again, then adds, "Didn't sound so well educated as you."

Daniel crosses his arms and looks at her, and she thinks he's amused, but she's not sure. Not even sure why he would be. He says, "This is not a lot to go on."

1:33.

"Oh!" Zoe suddenly remembers. "His license plate is HDP . . . ahm . . . I think it was 374. No. 347. Definitely. I think."

"No helpful logo on the door? Like a company name? 'Don't like my driving? Call . . .'?"

Zoe shakes her head.

"Parking sticker?"

Again, she shakes her head.

"What kind of car?"

"I don't know. Silver something-or-other. Not a truck. Not a van. Just a regular car. Not brand-new. Not obviously old. Don't you have a friend on the police force who can run a trace on the license number?"

He's just looking at her. Apparently he doesn't think this is as brilliant a suggestion as she does.

She explains her reasoning. "Private eyes on TV always have helpful friends on the police force."

"Yeah," he points out, "and they also come with their own theme music and commercial breaks."

"No police friends?" she presses.

"Nobody who can get me the information in five minutes."

1:34.

Daniel amends that to, "Four minutes." He says, "Why don't you give me more details about how the robbery goes down. How many customers in the bank?"

"Maybe a half-dozen?" She tells him, "The guard is pretty generally useless." She feels guilty as soon as she says it, taking into account that he, also, dies more often than not. A close second only to Daniel. She continues, "When you're not there to set him off, I'm guessing maybe the robber suspects one of the tellers has pressed the silent alarm. One of them is a bit jittery about the whole armed robbery thing. The robber shoots her sometimes, too." She's thinking of the William-Henry-Harrison-coin teller, the one who squealed upon seeing the hold-up note.

"Which teller?" Daniel asks.

"Second from the right."

Daniel points out to her, "They aren't always at the same stations."

Zoe supposes this makes sense. She sighs at yet another description called for. "Kind of cold. And snooty. Has a tendency to look down her nose at you." She considers, then amends this to, "Well, at me."

Daniel looks as though he's fishing in his memory, and coming up with nothing.

Zoe adds, "Curly auburn hair pulled back from her face with a hairband . . . green eyes. Teal-colored glasses . . ."

"Charlotte?" Daniel interrupts incredulously. "The robber shoots *Charlotte*?"

Zoe doesn't remember seeing the woman's name. She's about to say, *Well, yeah, if Charlotte is the one with the reddish hair and the curls and the glasses.* But Daniel is looking so distressed at the thought of her getting shot, Zoe forgoes the snarkiness. He didn't react that openly to news of his own death. She says, "Sorry. Friend of yours?"

She has no right, Zoe tells herself, to feel jealous.

But she does.

1:35.

However, Daniel is shaking his head. "Not really. It's just . . . sad. Charlotte only recently suffered a miscarriage."

This seems pretty personal information to have—for someone who describes their friendship as "not really." Zoe presses on, observing, "But you're close enough she told you about it."

"No," Daniel says. "But she was very obviously about six months pregnant. And then she was very obviously not."

Zoe supposes private investigators need to be observant like that. *Poor Charlotte,* she thinks, willing—under the circumstances—to forgive the teller's snappy impatience, her peeved-at-the-world attitude.

Daniel brings Zoe back to the matter at hand. "So the guard pretty much doesn't notice the robber . . . ?"

Zoe nods.

". . . till Charlotte . . . ?"

"Draws everybody's attention by squealing," Zoe finishes. "And once he starts shooting, the robber just . . . keeps on shooting people."

Daniel is considering all of this, no doubt trying to picture the timing, everyone's positions. He asks, "So he comes by car . . . ?"

If he's hoping that if he sneaks up on the question, she'll be able to come up with more details about the vehicle, he's sadly mistaken. She says, "He parks it across the street, in front of the card shop. There's a woman with a baby who's parked directly in front of the bank. She comes back to the car about 1:36."

Daniel starts to ask, but then apparently decides he doesn't want to know their fates. He's watching the digital readout on the phone, evidently having finally run out of questions.

Zoe hopes that means he's working on a plan. She tells him, "The rain starts at 1:23. I estimate the robber arrives at 1:29. With you not in the bank, it's 1:37 when he'll start shooting. Earlier, otherwise."

"You're pretty good for someone without a timepiece."

She shrugs.

Just as the time changes to 1:36.

Zoe asks, "So what should we do?"

"I suppose it doesn't make any difference *who* he is. The

111

important thing is to stop him before he gets into the bank."

"How do we do that?"

"Stop saying *we*. You'll stay here. Inside."

On the one hand, she's relieved to be authoritatively told she's to remain out of it. No chance of getting shot again. And she will *not* take that chance again. On the other hand . . .

"Except," Zoe reminds him, "you won't remember any of this conversation."

"That's a real pain in the butt," Daniel says.

"Yeah, tell me about it. How do I win you over real fast?"

"*Armadillo* helped. As did your knowing I was carrying a gun." He hesitates. "I hope this doesn't sound as though I'm the kind of person who enjoys other people's fear . . . but it was pretty convincing to see how you were so clearly afraid of me and yet just as clearly felt you absolutely needed to talk to me."

"Can't do that again," Zoe points out. She's amazed she *could* have been that distrustful of him. She's also amazed at how vulnerable he makes her feel, and how feeling vulnerable . . . somehow . . . doesn't feel bad.

Daniel finishes, "And the fact that you were unflinchingly honest about your earlier . . ." —he drums his fingers on the folder—". . . troubles."

"OK," Zoe says.

"Oh. Got it: Mention the trust fund papers. Tell me that Nick Wyand"—Daniel nods his head upstairs to indicate the lawyer he was visiting—"finished by saying, 'Give my love to your mother,' and that kind of creeped me out, Nick being . . . well, Nick."

Zoe says, "I have no idea what you just said, but fine."

Daniel says, "Try not to let me get sidetracked . . ."

112

Zoe snorts and says, "Yeah, right."

"No, really. Tell me: 'We discussed this already. There's no time.'"

The cell phone shows 1:37.

Daniel glances door-ward. His voice comes out small, and somewhat shaky. "Surely," he says, "there has to be something—"

Zoe shakes her head. "Next time," she tells him.

He's very obviously fighting the inclination to be moving, to be doing something. But he takes her at her word. He picks up his phone and tries to hand both it and her folder to Zoe.

"Doesn't make any difference," Zoe says. "The folder will be back with me at 1:16 whether I'm holding it now or not. And the phone will once again be with you."

Not being as familiar with the the ins and outs of playback as she is, Daniel nods slowly, taking her word for that, too.

From outside there's a noise which they both recognize can only be the sound of gunfire.

If Daniel had any lingering doubt, this settles it. She thinks he looks pale and scared and young. He, too, she realizes, is used to being self-sufficient, and doesn't quite know how to handle being dependent on someone else.

She really, really doesn't want to try again. She also knows Daniel will not forgive himself—and, by extension, her—if she doesn't. "See you," Zoe tells him just as door 1C bangs open, and M. Van Der Meer sticks his head out, demanding, "Hey! Did you hear—"

Daniel, still sitting on the bottom step with his phone and her folder on his lap, raises a hand to her in farewell as Zoe puts her arms around herself and says, "Playback."

CHAPTER 11

Time resets to 1:16.

Zoe holds onto her folder as she runs to Independence Street. If Daniel was persuaded to believe her because of her openness about her psychiatric record, then open she will be. She mentally reviews all the things that Daniel said made him inclined to trust her, desperate to maximize the time they'll have to work on the actual solution to the bank robbery. She's thinking and she's running, and she comes close—but not *that* close—to the biker guy and his Chihuahua. Certainly not close enough to justify how he scoops the small animal up to the safety of his arms as though saving its life, overreaction evidenced by the way he still has time to give Zoe the finger before she passes them.

Once again she dashes into the converted-into-offices Fitzhugh House. Once again she slams the front door. And once again she's able to glower away the nosy man from office 1C.

She's ready and waiting on the landing as Daniel starts down the stairs from the 2A office of Nicholas Wyand, Attorney-at-Law.

"Hi Daniel, I'm Zoe. I'm supposed to say *armadillo* to you to let you know that I'm an OK stranger to be talking to you. Can we sit here on the landing for a few minutes? I know you've just been talking trust fund business with Nick, who's apparently a bit creepy, at least when it comes to your mother. Normally, I'd be afraid of you because you're carrying a gun, but I know I can trust you, and I hope you feel you can trust me."

Perhaps she's been a bit too succinct. Daniel looks somewhat taken aback by her rapid-fire words, maybe even a bit uneasy. She stops short of handing him the folder full of psych evaluations, judging the timing for that might be off.

Zoe takes a deep breath. "Sorry," she says, and repeats it for good measure. "Sorry. I need to talk to you about something very important. Please."

"*Who* are you?" he asks, even though she's covered that already—not a good sign.

"Zoe," she repeats, trying not to sound rushed, or impatient. "We met before, in a different life, sort of, and you told me about how *armadillo* was sort of a code word for you, when you were a kid, and so you told me to use it . . . to sort of introduce myself to you . . ." She drifts off, but is unable to stop tacking on one last, ". . . sort of."

He's looking more confused than apprehensive, and Zoe supposes that's a good sign. Though he still hasn't sat down. He tries to sort his way through her words. "We met, so I told you how to introduce yourself to me . . . ?"

"We *sort of* met," Zoe explains.

"In a different life?"

"Well, in a *sort of* different life."

Daniel's patience snaps. "Which, I gather, is *sort of* different from reincarnation? Because I don't believe in reincarnation. Oh, wait. No doubt you already knew that." His tone has just veered off into snarky.

Zoe says, "I think we got off to a bad start."

"This time or last time?" Daniel asks. He has made his way from befuddlement to wariness to annoyance to sarcasm in sixty seconds flat.

She has messed up *everything*. For someone who only this morning felt relatively satisfied with her ability to deal with people, she is amazed at how quickly things have sped out of control. Zoe sits down on the bottom step of the upper flight because her legs, once again, have gone rubbery. She looks directly at him, into his blue eyes.

He shakes his head, puts on his sunglasses, and starts down the stairs.

Her overeagerness to get started has ruined everything. That one housemother would not be able to refrain from a self-satisfied *I told you so.*

Too impulsive.

Except, of course, for those times she's paralyzed by indecision.

Zoe rests her forehead in her hands, unable to watch him leave, and mumbles after him, "I don't know what to tell you. Except that what I need to talk to you about is important."

She hears the front door open.

And close. Rather forcefully.

What an idiot she is. Yet another wasted playback. And only two more to go.

She tries not to cry, not to feel sorry for herself. It isn't that she's tired from reliving these twenty-three minutes over and over, not exactly, not physically, because her energy level—like everything else—resets each time she returns to 1:16. But *emotionally* she feels battered.

116

Her mother, she's coming to realize, was right in her evaluation of Zoe. No wonder her father never came back for her once he recovered. Stupid, worthless, messing-up-everything loser that she is.

The floor below her creaks, and she figures M. the Designer has once again poked his head out of 1C to find out what is going on.

But it's Daniel's voice she hears: Daniel, who says, sounding irritated—either with her, or with himself, for not leaving when he had the opportunity to—"*What* is it you need to tell me?"

He crouches on the landing in front of her, but makes no effort to hide how exasperated he is. He's pushed the sunglasses up on his head—a signal, whether he means to proclaim it that blatantly or not, that he can easily pull them back down to block her off. She is on probation, so to speak, and he can leave at a moment's notice.

"Let's start over," he suggests.

"Yes. Please." She intentionally speaks slowly and—she hopes—calmly. "My name is Zoe. I know you're Daniel Lentini. I know you're a private investigator. We met once before in a past you don't remember. I know this sounds crazy—and I have the papers here to prove that I have been in the mental health system. But the truth is, I have a very limited ability to travel back in time. And it's precisely because that sounds so crazy that you gave me some key things to mention to you—to prove I *have* met you. Several times already."

His gaze flicks to the papers she's holding, but he doesn't ask to see them. Neither does he comment on the whole mental illness thing. He stands, and she winces at the thought that she's lost him. But he's only moving from crouching before her to sitting next to her. He sets down his envelope full of trust fund stuff, but it's within easy reach for him, ready to be snatched up again should he decide enough is enough. He asks, "So you keep reliving the same time over and over? Voluntarily?"

Ooh, good question. He's catching on despite himself.

She nods. "The same twenty-three minutes," she clarifies. "But only up to ten times. And this is attempt number eight. Which is why I was so . . . pushy."

"What's special about *this* twenty-three minutes?"

"There's an armed robber who's about to walk into Spencerport Savings and Loan." She's aware that it's just started raining, and she adds, "In six minutes. Depending on what we do next, either a few or a lot of people will get killed."

Daniel is looking at her seriously, which might mean he believes her, or might mean he's thinking, *Crap! Why didn't I run away from this psycho when I had the chance?*

She can't afford to go too fast, but she has just as much to lose by going too slow. She finishes, "In almost all cases, you were one of the first to die."

He's just watching her, waiting, not showing her what he's thinking.

"In the cases where you didn't die, you gave me those details—armadillo, trust fund, Nick Wyand is a bit creepy when it comes to your mom—so I could kind of bring you up to speed quickly. I think I probably tried too quickly."

Daniel nods, but she isn't sure whether it's to indicate *No kidding, too quickly*, or if he's telling her he believes her. She hopes it's evidence of the second case when he asks, "I couldn't just give you a business card on which I'd written—"

"No, I can't bring anything back with me."

Next he asks, "I take it we've tried calling the police?"

"We've covered this before," she tells him. "Doesn't help. You recognized the guy, but,"—she keeps talking as he opens his mouth to ask—"you didn't say his name out loud. And last time when we tried, we weren't able to figure who it was." Even though it sounds a bit rude to her, she says, "You sort of told me to keep you on track, and to cut you off—in the interest of time—from dead-end conversations."

Daniel isn't offended. "OK. Got it. Tell me what I need to know."

Hoping he isn't just trying to see how far her delusions extend, she tells him, "The robber parks across the street from the bank. There are about a dozen customers when he enters, but at least four or five of them leave before the shooting starts. The bank guard doesn't notice him till too late. Charlotte the bank teller " Zoe figures another proof at this point can't hurt and adds, "and, by the way, you told me how you deduced she had lost her baby—she does something to alert the robber that she's pressed the alarm, and that's when he starts shooting, if you *aren't* there. Otherwise, it's recognizing you that sets him off. This last time when we were planning, you talked about trying to intercept him."

"Before he goes in . . .," Daniel muses, as though once again coming to the conclusion that this seems the best option.

Zoe says, "He enters the bank at 1:29."

Daniel takes out his phone to check the time.

Zoe cranes her head to see. 1:25.

He's noticed her movement and is looking at her quizzically. "Two minutes ago, you knew exactly what time it was, and now you need to look?"

Zoe explains, "I don't have a watch or cell phone. Time always resets to 1:16. The rain starts at 1:23. These are things I've learned along the way."

He looks at her incredulously. "You're doing life-and-death maneuvering that requires precision timing without a watch or cell phone?"

"Well, not intentionally." Her own patience is fraying. She hesitates, unsure whether she is once again pushing too fast. But there's no time for niceties. She says, "If you believe me, we'd better get moving. Or even if you just think you *might* believe me."

He collects his envelope, stands, and sprints up the stairs.

Which looks more like running away from her than believing her.

But then he calls back down, "Creepy Nick might as well make himself useful."

Which is still not exactly a *yes*.

And yet, seconds later he's back, having traded his trust fund papers for an umbrella. Seeing her questioning look, he explains, "If I'm going to be hanging around outside the bank in the rain, I'll be less conspicuous if I'm carrying an umbrella as though I'm waiting for someone."

She's about to say *Good thought*, but he doesn't need her affirmation.

Seeing that she's followed him to the front door, he tells her, "You wait here."

"No," she says. "In case this doesn't work, I need to see what goes wrong." She assures him, "I have absolutely no intention of getting any closer to the bank than across the street."

"Still too dangerous," he objects.

"We've already covered this." Well, they have. They just didn't come to an agreement. She compromises. "I'll wait inside the card shop. There really isn't time to argue."

He hesitates.

"Eighth out of ten possible tries," she reminds him.

He's distracted by her papers, which she's left on the stairs: He's assuming they're as important to her as his are to him. They were. Once. She sees him glance from them up to the second floor.

"Don't need them anymore," Zoe says. Which is only partially true. She's trying to convince herself this is the time everything will work out, and she doesn't like the idea of abandoning her history here where a proven busybody like M. Van Der Meer can pry to his heart's content. But some things are more important than others.

On the front stoop, Daniel snaps open the umbrella, then angles out his elbow so she can take his arm and have cover from the rain. Which is sweet, but not exactly graceful for two people at a run.

Still, there's no car in front of the card shop yet, so they aren't too late.

Daniel must be anxious about the time, too. Outside the bank, he hands her his cell phone so she can keep track. It shows 1:28.

"Good luck," Zoe says—which sounds so clichéd, so bland, so hollow she thinks she'd have been better off saying nothing. What she wants to say is, *Keep yourself alive.* And, even as she ducks out from under cover of the umbrella to dash across the street, she regrets that she didn't. If anyone ever needed a remedial course on Not Getting Yourself Killed 101, it's Daniel. From the far curb, she turns back to call him a warning to please, please be careful, but she sees the silver car approaching.

It's on the wrong side of the street, which for a second confuses her, but in a moment she realizes there are no parking spaces in front of the bank because that's where the lady with the stroller has her car. The robber drives past, then makes a U-turn—strictly illegal (where's a traffic cop when you need one?)—and pulls to the curb right in front of where she's standing. Zoe turns her back to the street and opens the door of the card shop so as not to alert the robber that he is being watched, but not before pointing at the car in case *Daniel* needs alerting.

In the store, the woman with the hair rollers looks up from a display of souvenir-type caps that celebrate the Erie Canal: *Spencerport Canal Days, Colonial Belle Canal Cruise Tours, Sam Patch Packet Boat.* The woman smiles at Zoe and comments, "Nice weather for ducks."

Zoe, recalling the woman's former kindness and concern, smiles back but never takes her gaze from the man who is about to try to rob the bank. She watches him put on his Red Wings baseball cap and start across the street. Once he's safely facing away from the card shop, Zoe steps outside. At any sign that he's going for the gun, she assures herself, she can retreat—indoors or back to 1:16. But she needs to be outside, in case there's anything to hear.

Daniel, pacing in front of the bank with his umbrella as though impatiently waiting for someone, sees her and gives a tiny shake of his head for her not following instructions. But he can't do more without the possibility of drawing the approaching robber's attention to her. Instead, he pretends to just now take notice of the man and calls out, "Ricky Wallace."

This has to be purely for Zoe's benefit—an identification, should they have to go through this again—for there is little surprise and no warmth in Daniel's acknowledgment of the man.

122

As for the robber—Ricky Wallace, apparently—the friendliest thing that can be attributed to him is that when he gets to the sidewalk where Daniel is standing, he doesn't pull out his gun. He does, however, get right in Daniel's face. He's loud enough Zoe can hear every word. "Lentini, you son-of-a-bitch—you following me?"

From where she's standing directly across the street, Zoe can see Daniel's face clearly, and the back of Wallace's head. But Daniel is soft-spoken and the rain is muffling sound, so now that he's talking in a normal tone of voice, she can't hear him. Despite years of eavesdropping on resident evaluation meetings held behind closed doors at her various group homes, which have made her quite accomplished at extrapolating and filling in the blanks, she can't make out what Wallace is saying either—just, once in a while, a string of expletives.

Daniel continues to speak quietly and calmly, which Zoe finds remarkable, considering he's being sworn at by someone who has repeatedly shot and killed him.

Still, instead of mollifying Wallace, Daniel's composure seems to aggravate him even more. In a way, Zoe can empathize: There's nothing worse than trying to get a reaction from a therapist who only murmurs, *And why do you think you feel that way?* In any case, Wallace shoves Daniel, backing him up against the plate-glass window of the bank and shouting loudly enough that Zoe can catch: "Think you're better than me? You with your upscale East Ave. office, charging your five hundred dollars a day to ruin people's lives? Most of the people I know are lucky to clear five hundred in a week. What gives you the right (mumble) just because you been to some (mumble, mumble) college (mumble) . . ." Just as his words once more become unintelligible, he stops shouting and again shoves Daniel for emphasis, hard enough the bank window must rattle, for Zoe can see one of the customers look up, startled, before returning to filling out his papers.

Zoe has stepped out from the protective overhang of the card shop without even being aware of doing so, without even being aware of the rain running down her hair and molding her shirt to her body. *You have a gun*, she mentally reminds Daniel.

But, frustrating as it is, Zoe guesses she understands Daniel's reluctance; Wallace has been belligerent, but he hasn't exactly demonstrated unequivocal intent to harm anyone. Clearly, the *we've-lived-through-this-before-and-Wallace-was-about-to-kill-people* defense would not stand up in court.

Though this would still be better than getting killed, Zoe reflects.

She finds herself nostalgic for the good old days of Mrs. Davies's black-and-white Westerns, where—in the absence of due process of law—simple townsfolk *knew* who were the good guys and who were the bad guys, and gave the good guys a certain leeway.

Of course, in those same days before due process, the simple townsfolk would have hanged, burned, or stoned Zoe as a witch, or put her in chains and locked her in an insane asylum. All Zoe has had to put up with are unneeded medications that made her sluggish and prone to gain weight, tedious group therapy sessions, and well-intentioned if clueless counselors.

Daniel has gone from shaking his head to saying something Zoe still can't hear, but Wallace isn't buying any of it.

"Liar!" he shouts. He raises his arm and Zoe can guess that he's about to flat-hand Daniel in the face, to smack his head against—if not through—the glass.

124

Daniel swings the handle of his umbrella hard against the side of Wallace's head.

You've got a gun, Zoe thinks at Daniel, *and you're using an umbrella?*

Zoe is unaware of the card shop door opening behind her, when out steps the woman in the hair rollers. Maybe she's done with her card-shop needs, or maybe she's come to check up on poor-little-duck Zoe. But her timing is perfect.

Perfectly wrong.

As a witness, the woman was still inside the store for Wallace yelling at Daniel, for Daniel's unruffled replies, for Wallace shoving Daniel against the bank window—twice—and even for Wallace raising his hand with the how-much-more-obvious-can-you-get intention to pummel Daniel. All she is outside to see is Daniel's purely defensive swing of the umbrella.

"Hey!" Hair Roller Woman shouts. "Don't you hit that poor defenseless homeless man! He's gotta live, too."

Zoe can see the situation through Hair Roller Woman's eyes: Daniel, young, well put together, the picture of someone with all the advantages of life; Wallace, older, an edge of desperation to him, his raincoat a bit shabby, a bit dirty. Hair Roller Woman is assuming Wallace has tried to wheedle a buck-or-two handout from Daniel, and that Daniel, full of himself and disdainful of others' troubles, has heartlessly lashed out at him.

And what Hair Roller Woman has done is to distract Daniel, who for one brief second glances away from Wallace.

"Gun!" Zoe screams, even as Wallace's hand goes for his raincoat pocket.

Daniel is quick to tackle Wallace, but he is not acting on thorough information. Zoe told him Wallace is armed, but she had not thought to mention *where* he is carrying his gun. The way Daniel grabs hold of him to restrain his upper body, Zoe can tell that Daniel is assuming a shoulder holster, such as the one he himself is wearing.

Without even drawing his gun from his pocket, Wallace fires.

At a distance of fewer than six inches away, there is not a chance of his missing. Daniel doubles over, the umbrella dropped, his arms crossed over his midsection, but unable to stop the flow of blood spilling out between his fingers. As that other time in the bank, when Zoe was hit, the bullet has once again passed through Daniel—this time striking and shattering the bank window behind him.

Hair Roller Woman, finally realizing she has thoroughly misjudged what's going on, screams.

Wallace whips around and fires a second shot.

Zoe drops to her knees behind his silver car, her heart beating so hard she can't even tell if she's been hit.

Apparently not.

Not this time.

Hair Roller Woman, on the other hand, has fallen to the sidewalk beside her, face up in the rain, a single red dot on her forehead, almost like a Hindu woman's bindi. Was it her scream that caused Wallace to want her dead? Or, more likely, Zoe's warning shout? Has Wallace in fact realized there were two witnesses, or is Hair Roller Woman dead in Zoe's place?

Without knowing if Wallace has seen her, there is no telling whether he'll cross the street to come after her.

She desperately wants to be away from here. Her chest and shoulder ache from the memory of the other story line, the one in which she was shot. She does not want to die. But meanwhile, what of Daniel? If there's any chance he's still alive, she does not want to desert him. She will not be the brain-dead observer she was when her father was shot. There is no receptionist now.

Only Zoe.

And Zoe is determined not to abandon Daniel.

A glance at the cell phone he loaned her shows 1:33. Still lots of time. For good or ill.

She hears a third gunshot. More glass breaking. Now she can hear the screams from within the bank. She hopes this means Wallace has not fired a second shot at Daniel. Though she feels awful for thinking it, she hopes this means Wallace has turned his attention away both from this side of the street and from Daniel, returning to his Daniel-interrupted original plan to rob the bank.

Zoe flattens herself on the rain-wet sidewalk and tries to see beneath the car to what is going on, but she can't make out much of anything. So she gets to her hands and knees and scuttles toward the back of the car. The hood is lower than the trunk, but to get there would mean skirting around the dead Hair Roller Woman, and Zoe can't bring herself to look at her again. *My fault*, she thinks. *My direct fault she's dead.*

Her indirect fault about Daniel.

Zoe peeks over the trunk and sees that Wallace has kicked in a section of the broken window and stepped into the bank.

And, more than Zoe dared hope, Daniel is still alive. Wallace must have left him, not considering him a threat, not thinking it worth the time to finish him off when there's a bank that needs robbing. Unable to stand, Daniel is dragging himself away from the opening that was formerly a window, heading to the brick corner of the building.

With his left arm pressed against his stomach, still unsuccessful with slowing down the flow of blood, he has drawn his gun with his right hand. He uses the bricks to pull himself up to his feet. He has left a prodigious blood trail on the sidewalk, and Zoe tries her best to convince herself that it has been diluted and spread by the rain, that there is not really as much blood as there appears to be.

Daniel still alive changes everything. Zoe dashes out from the cover of the car and across the street, where she takes hold of Daniel by the shoulders and gets him to sit back down—he's resisting but unable to fend her off, which is not a good sign.

"You're supposed to be *inside* the card shop," he reprimands her from between teeth clenched in pain.

"I don't listen well," Zoe admits. That's something else housemothers have included in their reports.

Daniel grunts, either at what she's just said or because of the pain, but in any case he says, "Help me up."

"Just keep your head down," Zoe tells him. "Someone from the bank or the store must have alerted the police by now and they should be here any minute. And an ambulance."

Zoe is most fervently hoping for an ambulance. She is trying not to see the blood, and especially the wound from which it's coming, so she's concentrating on his face, which has gone very white. Somehow, that makes his eyes look bigger and bluer, almost like an anime character.

"Do you think," Daniel demands, "that when Wallace comes out of the bank and sees you here and me still alive, he won't shoot again?"

This seems a perfect reason for them to get out of there

straightaway, but Zoe can see Daniel isn't going to be able to move to cover anytime soon.

"Help me up," Daniel repeats, and this time Zoe does, letting him lean heavily on her, letting him bleed on her.

Inside the bank, Wallace has gotten hold of the bag of money he's made the tellers pass. The guard is lying on the marble floor, writhing in pain, and one of the bank managers is kneeling beside him in a position that partially blocks their line of sight to Wallace until Zoe helps Daniel to a higher vantage by standing.

She prays Daniel is a good shot. If he misses, or even if he hits but only wounds, she and Daniel will be clear targets for Wallace.

Still, what kind of person prays for someone's success in killing someone else?

Daniel takes a steadying breath, and fires.

And Zoe's prayer is answered: Wallace drops to the ground, as patently dead as Hair Roller Woman.

Wallace was a human being, and Zoe tries not to think, *Good riddance.*

Mostly, she's not very successful at this.

Daniel slips from Zoe's grasp until he is once more sitting, his back against the support of the bricks between the door and the window. He's shaking, which makes her fear he's going into shock. And he is—but apparently not the kind of shock she's worried about.

"I've never shot anyone before," he says, as though he owes her an explanation, as though that's the important thing. "Damn. Damn, damn, damn."

That he could be distraught about killing the man who was

trying to kill him . . . who may well . . . Zoe forces herself away from that train of thought. Daniel is *not* going to die. She is shaking, too.

Zoe takes account of the damage: Daniel is wounded, badly, but she fervently hopes not so badly as it appears. Not that she's an expert. But Dad survived—though there wasn't nearly this much blood when he was shot. Still . . . She tries to squelch the negative thoughts. Still, Daniel *has* to be OK. The bank guard is wounded, though conscious and quite vocal, which might indicate he is not as seriously injured as he thinks. Wallace is dead—and Zoe can't help but think, *No loss there.* Hair Roller Woman is dead, which she never was in any other version of this twenty-three minutes.

Zoe asks herself: Is this as good as she's going to be able to get it?

"Take the gun," Daniel tells her. His voice has become a reedy whisper. She can only hear him clearly because the rain has finally slowed to a drizzle.

"Why?" she asks, thinking she'd never be able to fire it. And that, in any case, the need for firing it has passed.

"Take the gun," he repeats, so softly she isn't even sure she really hears the words or if she's just guessing by the movement of his lips.

She puts her hand out and the gun falls into her grasp, and she realizes he didn't have the strength to set it down. And he didn't want it dropping to the sidewalk, potentially discharging.

Carefully she lays the gun down on the sidewalk next to her, hating the feel of the weapon, not even taking into account that it's sticky with Daniel's blood.

Sirens are wailing in the distance.

"You're going to be all right," Zoe assures Daniel, pulling him so that he is leaning against her rather than the wall for support.

And, for a moment or two, she even believes he might be.

There's no telling what he believes.

He rests his head on her shoulder and closes his eyes.

She could play back now, but she remembers the previous twenty-three minutes, when he comforted her when she couldn't stop crying, after she realized she'd almost given up on trying to save him because she hadn't trusted him, believing he himself was a bank robber. So she puts her arms around him and whispers, "Don't be afraid," and holds him close. And holds him close. And holds him close. Until long after she knows he's died.

But before 1:39.

She stands up. She stands clear of him. She puts her Daniel-bloody arms around herself, and she whispers, "Playback."

CHAPTER 12.

TIME RESETS TO 1:16.

Zoe tightens her hold on her folder, pure muscle reflex at this point, and starts running toward Independence Street when all she wants to do is curl into a ball and cry—even though she thinks of herself as not the crying type. Despite all the crying she did two playbacks past.

Meanwhile, her mind is churning on its own. *I hate this. Hate this. Hate this*, she is thinking. *How many times do I have to go through this same stupid damn thing?*

But she knows the answer. This time, and maybe once more. Then this twenty-three-minute interval will be closed forever. And she isn't making good progress as far as damage control. Each time she's relived it, she's learned things—but then everything else shifts and leaves her unable to use what she's learned, leaves her stumbling and falling. And taking Daniel with her.

She thinks again: These twenty-three minutes will be gone. Except for memories.

Always memories.

And regrets.

She arrives at the Victorian house. Not by any conscious effort, but because she's begun weaving with mental and emotional exhaustion, her shutting of the front door behind her is somewhat feeble. The door does not slam. M. Van Der Meer, Designer, has not been alerted that there is something snoop-worthy going on in his building's lobby.

Despite her distress, Zoe has made good time. No sign yet of Daniel. Too drained to go to the second floor to intercept him the moment he steps out of his attorney's office, or even to make it halfway up to the landing, Zoe sits on the bottom step to wait.

Somehow this position reminds her body, as opposed to simply her mind, of sitting on the sidewalk holding Daniel while he bled out.

Not now, she tells her body. There's no time for this.

Her body has ideas of its own.

There's a rapidly expanding balloon in her chest that's squeezing her heart, cutting off her breathing. Her hands, clasped together on her lap, are trembling. In an attempt to hold them steady, she wraps her arms around her knees. But now the palsy has spread to her arms. And her shoulders. And pretty much all of her. She lowers her head to her knees.

Don't cry, she commands herself.

She's never been good at taking direction. Even from herself, apparently. She releases her hold on her knees and puts her arms around her head to block out the world.

Between the balloon in her chest and her sobbing, Zoe is unable to catch her breath. She thinks of Rasheena, who has asthma and sometimes has to use an inhaler, and for the first time understands how this feels.

A gentle hand touches her shoulder.

Somehow she missed him coming down the stairs. Daniel is once more sitting next to her. "Are you hurt?" he asks. "Did you fall?"

Zoe shakes her head in her arm-pillow on her knees.

"Has something bad happened?"

Zoe is torn between thinking, *Oh boy, has it ever*, and wanting to point out to him that, as young as he might think she looks, he does *not* need to talk to her as though she's nine years old.

Instead of saying either of those things, she once more shakes her head.

She hasn't raised her face, so it takes him saying, "Here . . ." before she looks up and notices he is once again offering her the linen hankie, which is—once again—impeccably clean and ironed.

This is never going to work if she keeps wasting precious time. She takes the hankie and blows her nose.

He says, "I know you don't know me, but is there anything I can do to help?"

Yet again, she shakes her head. But this time she says, "I *do* know you. You're Daniel Lentini. And you're a private investigator. I came here to see you."

"Here?" he repeats.

"It's very complicated," she tells him.

"I can see that," he answers.

Won't he *stop* treating her like a child? Because it's easier to be annoyed at him than to face his death, she snaps, "Don't be condescending."

"I didn't mean to be." He waits a moment to see if she'll fill in any details. When she doesn't, he explains, calm and quiet: "I only meant, you said I couldn't help, but you also said you came to see me. And, then again, you came to see me someplace where I just happen to be visiting, not where I live or work. That sounds complicated to me."

"I'm sorry," she says, meaning for snarking at him. But once she's started, she can't stop. "I'm sorry, I'm sorry, I'm sorry, I'm sorry, I'm sorry . . ." She means for his dying. The first time. And the last time. And all the times in between. And she means for wasting valuable minutes on self-pity. But mostly she means for being the girl Mom thinks she is, for not being smarter, faster, braver, or whatever it is the situation requires from her that she just doesn't have. She's started sobbing once more, rocking like the autistic kids who sometimes pass through the home, and Daniel puts his arm around her. This time he asks, *"How* can I help?"

Can't he just stop being so damn nice?

"I saw you die," she tells him.

His eyebrows go up.

She changes that to, "I've seen you die. Repeatedly."

He's trying to work this out. "You mean . . . as in a dream? A vision?"

"As in time travel," she says. "Which I know sounds crazy."

He has the grace not to try to pretend otherwise.

She tells him, "There's a man you know, Ricky Wallace, who's about to walk into Spencerport Savings and Loan with a gun."

Daniel starts, "I was—"

And Zoe finishes, "—just on your way there. Yes, I know. With some trust fund stuff you picked up from Nick Wyand, who mentioned your mother right before you left, which put your teeth on edge. Every time you make it into the bank, Ricky Wallace shoots you. If you're not there, he shoots a bunch of other people. If you try to stop him on the street before he goes in, he shoots you. No matter how I play it back, it just stays bad. If I call the police, if I try to warn the bank guard. No matter what the hell I do, people die."

She wants to be shouting, yet she's sounding just like Rasheena again, wheezing and breathless, and she has to stop talking.

Daniel is looking a bit dazed at this onslaught of information.

Once she can speak again, Zoe continues, "Really, this is true. I've learned things about you as we've lived through these same twenty-three minutes over and over. You told me about how you and your parents had the code word *armadillo* in case they ever had to send a stranger to pick you up." She gives a bitter laugh. "I bet none of you anticipated anybody as strange as me."

"*Are* you a stranger who's trying to pick me up?" Daniel asks.

"No!" she protests. "No. That's not . . ." But then she sees his sweet, sad smile, and she thinks that, paradoxically, his joking might well mean he's taking her seriously. Or maybe it just means he's taking her as seriously demented.

Speaking of which . . . she holds the folder out to him. "These are my mental health records," she says. "The doctors thought I might be schizophrenic, or at least delusional, when I told the truth about my ability to play back time."

His eyes do go a bit wide at that reference to schizophrenia, but he doesn't reach for the folder.

She finishes, "But then when I lied and said I was making it up, they thought *that* made more sense, was more normal."

Daniel says, "You mentioned twenty-three minutes."

"That's as far back as I can go," Zoe says. "And only up to ten times. This is time number nine."

"That doesn't leave a lot of room for error," Daniel points out.

"It does not," Zoe agrees. He's accepting her story, and she can no longer say whether this is even what she wants anymore. She is beginning to consider a new plan: If they should fail again on this ninth playback—and she has no reason to believe they won't—then for the final trip through this twenty-three minutes, she will keep him out of the bank. She cannot risk a tenth failure in which he'll die. She'll find a way to engage him in conversation long enough to keep him out of Ricky Wallace's sights *without* telling anything about what she knows. Maybe she can sidetrack Daniel with some story—perhaps she can say she wants to hire him to find her father. Even though, in truth, she knows how to reach Dad as surely as Dad knows how to reach her. It's just that neither of them has bothered to. Not since Mom took that one shot at him. Zoe has suddenly become an expert in shots fired, and has no sympathy for someone who deserts his family after only one—even if you throw in that his daughter has been officially certified as wacko. But she can use looking for her father as an excuse for approaching Daniel. Then, when the shooting starts in the bank, Daniel will consider it coincidence rather than design that kept him out of there. This way he won't feel guilty about the others dying so he could live, which she knows would weigh on his soul.

The guilt for that choice will be solidly where it belongs: on her.

Daniel asks her, "What have we learned?"

What have we learned?

Besides that nothing works . . . ?

"Oh!" An important thought crosses her mind. "He carries his gun in the right-hand pocket of his raincoat, not . . ." She drums her fingers in the area of her upper ribs, beneath her left arm, to indicate where, on his body, Daniel wears his. "That time you tried to stop him before he went into the bank, he managed to shoot you because you tried talking him out of it and you waited too long to draw your own weapon."

She means this as a cautionary tale, but, "Wow," Daniel says. "This all sounds so . . ."

She's expecting him to say *far-fetched*.

Instead, he finishes, ". . . incompetent of me."

"Oh," she says, and this time it feels as though her heart itself is ballooning out. "No. No, Daniel. You have been so brave." She wants to say more, but her expanding heart closes her throat.

And Daniel gives a little roll of his eyes at what she *has* said.

She mentally makes her plan into A Promise: She will *not* let him face Wallace on attempt number ten. She swallows hard and continues speaking. "I think Charlotte the bank teller freaks out and hits the alarm button, which is why Wallace shoots when you're not there. When you *are* there, he recognizes you. The time I saw this happen, you didn't say his name, but he obviously knew you could identify him. You . . . kept him busy . . . and the bank guard killed him just as . . ." The image is still too clear. She can't speak it. "The guard killed him too late."

She sees that Daniel understands perfectly well what she hasn't said.

Unexpectedly, he tells her, "Ricky Wallace isn't really that bad a guy. You've got to feel sorry for him."

"*What?*" Zoe snaps. "No, I don't. *What?*"

Daniel says, "His wife hired me to prove he was having an affair. Which she guessed because he'd moved all the money out of *their* account into *his* account. Which she found out when she tried to do the same thing to him. The divorce cleaned him out, and then his girlfriend left him."

138

OK. Well. "Still . . .," Zoe says.

"Still," Daniel agrees. Slowly, working this out in his head, he says, "So it sounds as though I need to go into the bank . . . try harder to talk him out of this plan of his . . . try to keep Charlotte calm . . . keep the bank guard informed . . ."

A voice she doesn't recognize demands, "Are you crazy?"

Daniel and Zoe both turn to look at the doorway of room 1C. Nosy M. Van Der Meer, Designer, has been listening with the door open a crack, and now he throws it fully open.

Zoe supposes that she *had* been crying rather loudly. It's no wonder she attracted his attention. She holds the folder up and explains, "Well, the doctors *thought* I was, but, really—"

"Yeah, yeah, I heard all that, sweetheart," M. Van Der Meer says to her. This is the first time she's really looked at him. He's dramatic in both looks and speech, with red eyeglasses that absolutely do not complement his purple tux jacket. He tells Zoe, "I'm not talking to you." To Daniel, he says, "Those things she said about you that she couldn't otherwise know? They're correct?"

Daniel nods.

"Fine. So she's got that part right." He goes from reasonable and composed to strident. "So are you out of your freaking mind to actually consider traipsing into that bank? What are you, the poster child for second-party suicide?"

Daniel considers. "Well, not so much *traipsing* . . ."

"Whatever." Van Der Meer dismisses Daniel's word-quibbling with a theatrical flourish of his hand. "This Wallace guy has it in for you no matter what? Bank robbery or no?"

Daniel says, "I really appreciate your concern—"

"Yeah, yeah," Van Der Meer interrupts. He suddenly grins at

Daniel. "By the way, I *am* the stranger interested in picking you up that your parents warned you about. My name is Milo." He puts out his hand and Daniel goes ahead and shakes it, though looking a bit tentative. "Have you at least considered wearing a disguise?"

Daniel starts, "There's no time—"

Zoe finds herself siding against Daniel. "Even if it just slows Wallace down a bit from recognizing you right away. At least take off the jacket. Wallace is all into thinking that you think you're better than he is because of your money."

"My what?" Daniel asks.

"Your expensive clothes, your privileged background, your Ivy League education . . ."

The way he's looking at her, she can tell she's suddenly losing him.

She suspects she's gone from uncanny accuracy to totally wrong. She hastily explains, "That's what Wallace said. He's not right?"

Daniel shakes his head without explaining where, exactly, he feels Wallace's description to be inaccurate. But he does take off his jacket, which *is* an expensive one, with an Italian label. Of course, now his gun holster is in plain view.

"Here." Milo takes off his purple jacket and trades it for Daniel's subdued gray one. "Even though," Milo points out, eyeing Daniel appreciatively, "you're *much* broader in the shoulders."

Daniel still looks apprehensive, but he slips on the jacket, which is snug, but not so much so as to call attention to it.

Milo hands over his red glasses. "They're not prescription or even readers—just plain glass, to make me look more professional. They should do a credible job of toning down your baby blues."

Zoe has no idea why Milo thinks red glasses make him look professional, or why someone who wants to look professional would wear a purple jacket. But Daniel puts on the glasses.

They're kind of cute, in a geeky kind of way, making Daniel look younger, but studious. More relevant, they *do* somewhat obscure the blueness of his eyes. Hopefully Wallace will note the clothes more than the face.

Milo steps forward and musses Daniel's hair, to try to further change his looks. "Ooh, good hair is good hair," Milo laments. "Maybe we could cut it, shame as that would be . . ."

For that, there's definitely no time. Zoe sees that it's raining, and she has no idea how long ago that started.

"The card shop across from the bank," Zoe says, "they sell caps. What time is it?"

"Don't you have a cell phone?" Daniel and Milo ask simultaneously.

She growls at them in exasperation, though Daniel can have no idea how often he's asked her that question. He informs her, "One twenty-four," sounding a bit bewildered at her strong reaction to what must strike him as a totally reasonable question.

"Wallace pulls up in his car at one twenty-eight," Zoe tells them, "and enters the bank at one twenty-nine. After that, we only have ten minutes."

Both men nod at her, acknowledging the necessity to get moving.

"Thank you," Daniel says to Milo, though Zoe suspects he still has his doubts. "Give us three minutes, then call the police and tell them you overheard someone talking about a bank robbery."

"Come back safe," Milo says, blowing an air kiss at them.

Well, Zoe suspects—at Daniel.

They don't bother with an umbrella this time. But they *do* bring their papers, which might make the two of them look like legitimate bank customers. Her folder is pretty sodden by the time they get to the card shop, and Daniel's trust fund envelope isn't doing much better.

Zoe goes to the display of Erie Canal caps and grabs the first one her hand touches, a blue one that proclaims *Sam Patch Packet Boat*.

The older man who appears to be the manager of the store glances their way disapprovingly, since Daniel is trying on the hat with wet hair, but he doesn't actually protest.

"Fine," Zoe tells Daniel, tucking his hair under the brim so it doesn't show.

Daniel takes out his wallet as he approaches the counter, but the woman who was leaving the store the first time Zoe went in, all those many lifetimes ago, is having something wrapped. And now she asks, as the manager is about to seal the box, "Did you take off the price sticker?"

"I believe I did," the manager says.

"Are you *sure* you did?" the customer insists.

Daniel glances at the other clerk, the one close to Zoe's age, who's fully engaged in showing the woman with the hair rollers the difference between the white teddy bears with the brown *I ♥ Rochester, NY* t-shirts and the brown teddy bears with the white *I ♥ Rochester, NY* t-shirts. In any case, there's only one cash register.

While the manager is disassembling the tissue wrapping to demonstrate to the customer that there's no price sticker on the gift

142

she's purchasing, Daniel rips the dangling price tag off his cap, then tosses thirty dollars onto the counter, which would cover the price even if New York State's sales tax were thirty-five percent. Which it isn't. Yet.

The manager is annoyed. "If you could just wait your turn for two minutes . . .," he starts.

"I can't," Daniel tells him, taking hold of Zoe's arm and marching her out the door.

The man's voice follows them, complaining, "This is too much." He couldn't sound more irritated if he were saying it was too little. "I'll get your change *once I—*"

And then the closing of the door behind them cuts him off.

Zoe mutters, "Consider it a tip for outstanding service."

But she does remember how he tried to ensure the safety of everyone in the store, the time she announced she could see Wallace had a gun.

Still on the card-shop side of the street, Daniel tells her, "Stay here."

She wants to. More than anything else, she wants to huddle safe in the doorway of the card shop and *not* get shot.

"You need me," she tells Daniel. "And," she adds as he starts to open his mouth to protest, "don't waste time arguing. We've discussed this. Twice already."

Well, they have.

Sort of.

Daniel shakes his head. But accepts what she's said.

The two of them cross the street and walk up to the bank, with Daniel still holding Zoe's arm. No doubt he can feel her shaking.

"What's your name?" he asks her, and she realizes she hasn't said, not this time. She hopes she hasn't left out any other, more crucial information.

"Zoe," she tells him. Then, for the first time, she adds her last name. Not that she has real hopes for this relationship to continue past this crisis. She only hopes *they* can outlast this crisis. But . . . just in case. "Zoe Mahar."

"Zoe," he starts, looking directly at her, which she fears—red glasses or not—makes her IQ drop twenty points. But something sidetracks him, causes him to change intention before finishing what he was about to say. Instead, he suddenly asks, "How old are you?"

She hesitates, then goes for the truth. "Fifteen. Almost sixteen," she tells him.

And then—after all the wildly fantastical, impossible-seeming things she's told him through all these versions of this long, long afternoon—*then* he looks skeptical. He says, "OK." But he says it just the tiniest smidgen of a bit too slowly.

"I *am*," she protests. "Have I *ever* lied to you?"

Unexpectedly, he out-and-out laughs. "*Ever?*" he repeats. "Isn't the whole point of this that you can remember, but I can't?"

Zoe does not laugh. She answers her own question. She says, "I have not."

That immediately wipes the grin off his face. He nods and says, "I'm sorry." But she isn't clear whether he means he's sorry he doubted her, or he's sorry she's only fifteen. Both would be nice. But she suspects the first is all she can really hope for.

Once again he says, "Zoe," speaking all slow and earnest. "When I tell you to move, I want you to move."

What he's saying is he doesn't want her standing anywhere near him once Wallace is in the bank.

"I understand," she says.

Which is not exactly the same as *OK*.

They walk into the bank. There is a big shiny clock on the wall, so Zoe doesn't need to keep asking the time, which is a relief. It is currently 1:27, and that is *not* a relief. Within the next sixty seconds, Wallace will be cruising down the street, looking for a parking space.

But meanwhile, the guard looks at them as though they are the least interesting people in the world.

"May I help you?" the teller at the far end of the row asks.

Daniel indicates they'd prefer to talk to Charlotte.

The hat-and-glasses-and-purple-jacket disguise, thrown together as it is, at least causes Charlotte to do a double-take. Then she smiles—something Zoe wasn't convinced she *could* do—and says, "Mr. Lentini." Her gaze strays to the souvenir cap. "Or is it Captain Patch?"

Zoe finds herself inordinately pleased that, despite the flirty tone, it's *Mr. Lentini*, not *Daniel*.

"Hello, Charlotte," Daniel says, as though they have all the time in the world, which—Zoe tells herself—is because Daniel doesn't want to spook Charlotte, not because he's flirting back or anything.

Charlotte even turns her smile onto Zoe, now that Zoe is with Daniel. Then she asks him, "Is this one of your brother's friends?"

Daniel has a brother?

It must be a younger brother, Zoe determines. The normally sucking-on-a-lemon-faced Charlotte is insinuating Zoe is too young to be a friend of Daniel's. OK, well, Zoe thinks Charlotte is too *old* to be a friend of Daniel's.

145

For some reason, Charlotte's question has stymied Daniel, who looks momentarily flummoxed, then says, "No," in a tone that's a strong hint that the question is somehow inappropriate. Then he adds, "Ms. Mahar is my client."

"Oh." Charlotte looks unconvinced. But she gets over it. She breezily adds, "Sorry. So, how can I help the two of you today?"

Daniel moves in closer and lowers his voice so as not to let anyone else overhear. "Don't become alarmed," he says.

Immediately, Zoe can see that Charlotte is not good at following instructions. Her eyes go all wide. This is verification of what Zoe has suspected all along. *Oh yeah*, Zoe thinks, *she's going to press the panic button as soon as she sees what Wallace is up to.*

And she's going to be so obvious about it, Wallace will see.

Zoe supposes they're lucky Charlotte hasn't pressed it at Daniel's words.

He continues to speak, his voice calm and soothing. He has put his rain-soggy trust-fund-stuff envelope down on the counter. Zoe is still holding her own paperwork, though she surmises the forms and printouts have probably melded together into one solid block of wet pulp: the ones saying she's delusional, the ones saying she's a liar, the ones saying she's too impulsive for her own good. Daniel now lays both his hands flat next to his envelope, and Zoe realizes this is deliberate: In case Charlotte knows or suspects he carries a weapon, this is meant to demonstrate—if this is what is making Charlotte anxious—that he's not a threat, that reaching for his weapon is the furthest thing from his mind. He asks Charlotte, "You know I'm a private investigator, right?"

She nods, still looking apprehensive.

"I need your help." Meanwhile, he has shifted slightly so he can

146

catch the bank guard's attention, and he motions for him to join them at the counter.

Can you move a little slower? Zoe thinks at the man as he strolls in their direction.

"Some trouble here, Mrs. Yeager?" the guard asks, addressing his question to Charlotte, despite the fact that it was Daniel who summoned him. He has his name on the lapel of his uniform shirt: Bobby Something-or-other-that-has-too-many-consonants-and-ends-in-*ski*. Zoe spares a thought for the feeling that *Bobby* is not a suitable name for anyone whose age is represented by more than one digit.

Moving slowly and carefully, as he did for Zoe that one time back at the Fitzhugh House, Daniel takes out his private investigator ID from its new home in the pocket of Milo Van Der Meer's jacket. Now he sets it on the counter and says, "I have reason to suspect an armed robber is about to enter the bank."

If Zoe thought Charlotte's eyes were big before, now they look about to pop right out of her face.

Daniel continues: "The police have been notified and are on their way. You can go ahead and press the silent alarm now if that makes you feel better, but it's superfluous, and the important thing is you need to keep calm once the man enters."

Bobby, who is at least twice as old as Daniel is, looks . . . perhaps not entirely convinced, but certainly as though he's more inclined to believe Daniel than he was to believe Zoe. He's wearing what he probably thinks of as his *professional* face, which looks pretty contemptuous of just about everything. He asks, "What about locking the door so the guy can't get in?"

Daniel points out, "OK, but he would just come back some time when you weren't expecting him. Besides . . . don't look now, but too late."

Not one of them does a good job with following that direction.

Daniel grips Zoe's arm to keep her from whipping around. At least Charlotte was facing in that direction already, and it's the guard's job to watch everybody. So perhaps Wallace hasn't realized anything is wrong. In any case, nobody's ducking, so Zoe supposes he doesn't look ready to open fire.

Bobby has angled himself so he can still see Wallace even while he talks to Daniel and Charlotte. He nods his head toward Daniel and asks Charlotte, "So you know this P.I.?"

Zoe, watching Charlotte since she isn't allowed to turn to face the door, sees Charlotte force herself to look away from Wallace. "Mr. Lentini?" she asks. "Of course. He's Pete's brother."

There's a flash of annoyance on Daniel's face, which makes Zoe question her earlier surmise that the brother must be younger. From her experience, it's usually the older family member everyone knows and to whom the younger is always compared, and for one second, that's how Zoe interprets Daniel's displeasure.

Then Bobby asks, incredulously, "Crazy Pete?"

And that's definitely more than annoyance in Daniel's expression now.

Immediately, Bobby tries to backtrack. "Sorry. Sorry, that was not called for. But . . ." He's looking at Charlotte with a not-very-subtle expression that seems to be asking, *Can we trust Crazy Pete's brother?*

Zoe, who had begun to feel she was an expert in all things Daniel, has no idea what to make of this conversation, except that it seems to be going pretty far afield from *a man with a gun has just entered the bank*. She has to work hard not to turn to see what that man with a gun is doing while they are huddled here talking, and she can only surmise that he's biding his time, waiting for the right opportunity.

Bobby is wearing a sucking-on-a-lemon expression so similar to Charlotte's usual look, it's as though he's been taking lessons from her. He says, "But, anyway . . . I can't arrest this guy just on your suspicion." Still, he looks inclined to concede that Daniel—crazy brother Pete notwithstanding—appears a more upstanding citizen than Wallace does. Zoe, however, is obviously a different matter. "And what's with the kid?"

Kid?

Daniel says, "I believe she and Ms. Yeager are in especial danger. Charlotte, I recommend you take Ms. Mahar toward the vault room as though you're bringing her to put that folder of hers into a safe deposit box."

This sounds less dangerous than being in this room, but the situation is too complicated for Zoe to know if she's feeling relief or anxiety that Daniel is making arrangements to keep her away from him. Not that she has a good track record for keeping him safe.

In any case, Charlotte is saying, "That is entirely against regulations," and even Bobby has grown suspicious again, asking, "Why *that* room? Is there something there you're hoping to get into?"

Daniel shakes his head at both of them. "I'm not saying to bring her *into* the vault area. There are those side privacy rooms for people who need time to sort through their belongings. *That's* where I want you to go." Specifically to Bobby he says, "I'm just trying to keep the two of them out of harm's way."

Charlotte says, "We should ask Mr. Bennington," by which Zoe takes her to mean one of the managers.

But even Bobby is shaking his head.

Zoe sneaks a peek in Wallace's direction. He's at the table with the deposit/withdrawal slips, obviously killing time waiting for the guard to step away from the tellers. But he's looking fidgety, and surely that's not a good sign. At least he isn't going for the low table with its COMPLIMENTARY COFFEE FOR OUR CUSTOMERS. Caffeine is probably the last thing in the world he needs.

"No time for that," Bobby decides, dismissing the idea of asking for advice or permission from the bank manager. "Ring the silent alarm and take her."

"But . . .," Charlotte starts.

"On my authority," Bobby tells her.

From Charlotte's face, she's trying to work out whether he *has* this authority, but her desire to get out of there overrides her concern for bank protocol. She says, "This way, Miss Mahar," and indicates she'll meet Zoe at the far end of the counter, where a waist-high railing separates the more public area of the bank from the behind-the-teller-counter area and the vault.

Zoe hesitates, feeling as though she's President William Henry Harrison's personal physician, advising the president, *Yeah, sure, go have fun with that inauguration speech thing. Good luck with the cold and the rain. I'll meet you inside after it's over.*

She doesn't want to desert Daniel. But can she really do anything besides get in the way?

As she and Charlotte take their separate paths toward the vault room, Zoe glances at the wall clock. 1:33. Six more minutes.

And nobody's dead yet.

The railing is hardly high-security. Obviously, it's meant to keep the clueless from wandering where they're not supposed to, rather than to barricade against armed intruders. Zoe sees four solid-looking doors which she guesses are the rooms about which Daniel was talking. She wonders if they lock from the inside, and if they're bulletproof.

As Charlotte opens the gate in the rail to let Zoe in, Zoe attempts to be subtle about turning to glance over her shoulder around the bank.

Daniel and Bobby have stepped away from the tellers' counter: Daniel is making for the table in the waiting area where the coffee is set up; Bobby is heading toward the entrance as though to take up his usual post just inside the door—although his bearing is as stiff as if he's expecting to be shot in the back at any moment. They're giving Wallace *some* room, but they're also flanking him, positioning themselves so they can be ready to move fast.

As for Wallace, he has stepped forward, between the two of them, heading for the teller counter. Alarmingly, he has opted to start at this end—which of course he would in any case, to avoid the empty space left by Charlotte's walking away from her station near the other end.

At which point Charlotte, holding the gate open for Zoe, looks up, sees Wallace apparently heading straight for her, and calls out in obvious panic, "Mr. Lentini!"

Wallace, of course, does not assume there could be another

Lentini in the world besides the one with whom he has a grudge. Even before Zoe has time to finish thinking at Charlotte, *I always knew you were an idiot*, Wallace has spun around to face the direction Charlotte is looking.

And he's holding his gun.

Except this time, finally, Daniel has his gun drawn, too.

And so does Bobby.

Zoe spares the thought that a *good* person would not be thinking that she'd feel better about the standoff if only Wallace were aiming at Bobby rather than Daniel. Bobby is probably a perfectly nice guy. After all, he believed Daniel. He wanted Zoe and Charlotte to be safely in the back. True, he called Daniel's brother crazy, an insult Zoe finds particularly offensive, but she tells herself allowances have to be made for someone who's risking his life to save yours. Still, Zoe thinks she'd give anything for Wallace *not* to be aiming at Daniel.

Until Wallace *does* shift away from Daniel.

Because now, while he's still looking at Daniel, he's swung the gun around toward Charlotte and Zoe.

Be careful what you wish for. This was one of her mother's sayings. She'd generally add: *The universe has a way of coming around and biting you on the ass.*

Yeah. That's something this whole playback ability has shown Zoe time and again.

But she still thinks, *Oh crap.*

"Nobody's been hurt yet," Daniel points out, reasonable and conciliatory, trying to defuse the situation. "Nobody needs to get hurt."

And any of the bank's customers and employees who hadn't

noticed before what's going on, notice now. There are startled gasps, squeals, and expletives.

"Shut up!" Wallace shouts at everyone. "Anyone who picks up a cell phone is dead." Then he says, "Drop the guns, both of you, or the women die first. I even suspect one of you tellers has pressed the alarm, and you'll be picking your coworker's brains out of the wall behind her."

Charlotte grabs Zoe's left arm and is holding onto it in wide-eyed terror as though she's drowning and Zoe's arm is a lifeline.

Zoe tries to convince herself that it's only logical—after all, she can't help anyone if she's dead—but she feels selfish and cowardly for recognizing the fact that if Charlotte would just let go, *she* could put her arms around herself and play back time.

Except, of course, that Wallace is looking directly at her, too.

"Drop," Wallace repeats, emphasizing each word. "The. Guns."

Daniel holds his arms up and away from his body to indicate surrender. He sets his weapon down next to the coffee machine. Bobby, following Daniel's lead, puts his on the deposit/withdrawal slip stand.

The clock on the wall shows 1:35, which still gives Zoe four minutes, so she doesn't need to yank free of Charlotte—at least, not immediately. Surely Daniel and Bobby laying down their arms must have appeased Wallace. At least for the moment.

"You," he says to Daniel, and gestures for him to step farther away from the table.

Daniel does.

"And you," he says to Bobby. "Lock the door. And close the window blinds."

That doesn't sound good. Zoe remembers the time she watched

from the street, and the helpful witness told her there was a hostage situation in the bank.

"And the rest of you," Wallace yells, "I said *shut up*! Nobody needs to get killed if you just shut the hell up and do what I say!"

As a motivational speech, it leaves a great deal to be desired, but the noise level inside the bank drops to some very ragged breathing and a few whimpers.

And all the while Wallace's gun is still aimed at Zoe and Charlotte.

With his free hand, Wallace reaches into an inside pocket of his raincoat, and he pulls out a canvas bag, which he tosses at the teller closest to him. "Everybody else," Wallace says, "face down on the floor. Hands behind your heads."

Everybody? Unsure if that order includes them, Zoe looks at Charlotte to check her reaction.

Charlotte suddenly releases Zoe's arm and dives for the floor on the far side of the guard rail.

Before Zoe can lower herself down, she's aware of a blur of movement in her peripheral sight and she hears Daniel, sounding a bit frantic, say, "Don't—"

And then someone has grabbed Zoe by the ponytail.

"How many times do I have to say *shut up*?" Wallace demands, his voice shouting just inches from Zoe's ear because, of course, he's the one who has a fistful of her hair.

Daniel, who has risen to one knee, once again lowers himself to the floor.

"This one of yours, Lentini?" Wallace asks. "This your kid sister?"

Daniel shakes his head, and Wallace aims his gun at Charlotte. "This Lentini's sister?" he asks her.

154

Charlotte, too, shakes her head. "Just some stray he's taken on."

Not that it makes any difference, but Zoe resents how Charlotte has made her sound like a feral cat, with Daniel being the neighborhood crazy cat lady.

Still holding the sodden lump of her papers, Zoe wraps her arms around herself, wondering if the playback spell will work since Wallace has hold only of her hair.

Trouble is, she needs to say *playback* out loud. She can whisper. But will *any* speaking set Wallace off?

Before she can decide whether to take the risk, he spins her around, and now he has his arm wrapped around her neck, which is definitely too much contact for playback to work. "You'll still do," he tells her, which sounds ominous. She decides it's best not to wonder, *For what?*

"Keep it moving," Wallace orders the tellers as they take turns stuffing banded stacks of money into his bag.

Zoe can't squirm loose; she knows she can't. What she manages to do is to catch a look at the big wall clock. Only two minutes left till 1:39, and then she'll be stuck with this time, not able to go back to any part of it.

Story line closed. Forever.

As her gaze drops away from the clock, she sees Daniel is watching her from his prone position on the floor in an anxious, bewildered way. He mouths something, but she can't tell what. He glances at the clock, then back at her. Oh. The next time he silently tells her *Go now*, she gets it. He's telling her to play back. She realizes she hasn't told him—this time—about how she can't be touching anyone. She makes a tiny gesture, a flick of her fingers, toward Wallace's arm around her neck and mouths back at Daniel, *Can't.*

Does he understand?

Daniel shifts his attention to Wallace. "Let the girl go," he says. "A minor doesn't make a good hostage. You can't take her out of here. Cops will put out an Amber Alert, they'll go all-out to stop you, and they won't take any chances, they'll send a sniper, you won't even—"

Almost conversationally, Wallace tells him, "I *am* looking for an excuse to shoot you in the face, you do realize that, don't you?"

Even given her own situation, Zoe winces. That's just too reminiscent of the very first time.

"All the same," Daniel finishes, "I'd make a much better hostage."

Zoe refuses to allow herself to think about this, one way or the other.

Wallace considers. Or, more likely, pretends to. It's hard to say. He puts his gun up to Zoe's head, then points it at Daniel, then brings it back to Zoe. "Naw," he says. "I think I'll stay with her." To Zoe he says, "I'll even let you hold the money, how's that, little blue girl?"

Zoe has no expectation that Wallace will let her live beyond her usefulness in getting him out of the bank—despite Daniel's earlier assertion that Wallace is not all bad.

So this is it, she thinks. *I've finally fixed things. Daniel gets to live, and Charlotte, and Bobby, and the rest.*

It's not like she has a good life or anything. Nor much prospect for things improving in the future. She hadn't thought much about dying before today, but now she finds a bit of satisfaction in the idea that her dying will save others. However pointless her life has been, her death won't be meaningless.

Looking ready to cry, the last teller hands Zoe the bag, which has made its way back to this end of the counter.

156

"OK," Wallace says to bank guard Bobby, "you can unlock the door now, then stand out of my way. You're another one I wouldn't mind shooting."

"She's just a kid," Bobby protests on Zoe's behalf.

Wallace answers, "And if she behaves herself, she'll be fine."

Zoe doesn't believe this, and she doubts anyone else does.

Daniel, of course, cannot leave well enough alone. Although he knows not to sit up, and so remains belly-down on the floor, he says, "You're in a lot of trouble already." He keeps on talking even as Wallace starts to turn back to him. He just speaks more rapidly, saying, "But that's nothing to the trouble you'll be in for kidnapping a minor. The police outside—"

"There *are* no police outside," Wallace shouts. He's walked Zoe with him as he's approached Daniel, the gun held out before him.

Shut up! Shut up! Shut up! Zoe thinks at Daniel. If he gets himself killed now, that will negate her own meaningful death.

Wallace says, "None of the tellers had a chance to push the alarm. I was watching."

"It was pressed as you were first coming in," Daniel tells him.

Wallace has reached Daniel and has his gun aimed at Daniel's forehead, inches away. But Daniel's words have him worried. "No," Wallace insists. "There was no reason then—"

Daniel tips his head toward the window and urges him, "Look."

The arm Wallace has around Zoe's neck gives a spasm. He orders Bobby, "Open the blinds."

Bobby does as instructed.

Wallace says, "Shit!"

And it's only then that Zoe sees the police cars all over the street.

A man with a flak jacket and a megaphone calls out, "Put down your weapon and let's start working on a peaceful resolution to this situation."

Whether it was Charlotte pressing the alarm, or Milo Van Der Meer calling it in, the troops have been summoned.

"Shit!" Wallace says again. "Close the blinds!" Angrily, he shoves Zoe away from himself, so that she falls to the ground, dropping the bag of money. She skids on the smooth marble floor, and she ends up actually sliding into Daniel.

Go! Daniel mouths at her again.

It pains her to abandon him, to have him *watch her* abandon him. Even though that's what he's telling her to do. Even though they both know she can't help these people now. Even though she knows *they'll* all be stuck with this if she dies. She puts her arms around herself. It's 1:38, with the second hand closing in on the final seconds of the minute. This story line is spiraling down into total disaster, and she only has one playback left. She tells herself, *I can't risk Daniel.* It isn't like it's clear what they should have done differently. There are too many variables. She needs to keep Daniel out of the bank. She would rather not have to sacrifice Charlotte. And Bobby. And the teller who was crying because Zoe was being taken hostage. Not to mention the baby stroller woman outside.

But she can't risk Daniel.

For her tenth try, she needs to let them die so he can live. Her voice shaking for the treachery of it, she says, "Playback."

And.

Nothing.

Happens.

CHAPTER 13

THE MINUTE HAND OF THE CLOCK MOVES TO 1:39.

Now, *now* time is supposed to be up.

Unfair! Unfair! Unfair!

Zoe knows she counted the playbacks correctly. So all of a sudden the universe is changing the rules on her?

Daniel is looking at her quizzically. He whispers, so as not to alert Wallace, "Does it always happen like this? You jump to where you're going, but for the rest of us . . . ?" He lets his voice drift off because she has very obviously not jumped anywhere.

Zoe lets her arms drop to her sides. "No," she whispers back to him. "It didn't work."

"OK," he says. "What does that mean?"

"We must have taken more than twenty-three minutes." She's working it out as she speaks. "*This* clock is set manually. It must be a minute off from the cell phones, which use a satellite and are all the same. We have to wait a full twenty-three minutes from now before I can do another playback."

"To *here*?" Daniel's voice is louder than it should be. "Why would we want to come back to this?"

Which, of course, is the whole point.

One of the bank managers—Zoe thinks it's the one who, the time Bobby the guard was wounded, was tending him—goes, "Shhh!" at them.

159

Fortunately, Wallace has taken a time-out for a minor temper tantrum, so he hasn't noticed. He kicks over the display table with the deposit and withdrawal slips.

Zoe's breath catches, as Bobby's gun, which he had placed on the table, hits the ground . . .

. . . And slides on the highly polished floor, a fraction of a second too fast for Bobby to intercept, and into one of the managers' offices.

So, for good or bad, that's one weapon out of play. Daniel's is still on the low table with the coffee supplies. He can't reach it without getting up; Zoe can't reach it without going over Daniel.

And meanwhile . . .

"Hey!" Wallace has caught on that he has no time for irritability. At least not against inanimate objects. He kicks Daniel in the ribs. "Shut," he commands, "up." Then he says, "This changes nothing. Get up." He tugs on Zoe's right arm, the one that belongs to the hand that's still clutching the meaningless folder. She's halfway between kneeling and standing when he tells her, "Put that down, and pick up the money."

A plan—born of desperation and perhaps of watching a few too many action/adventure movies—begins to form in her mind. Zoe figures Wallace can only kill her once. Unless, of course, someone else in here has the playback ability—but, if someone does, she'll never know. In any case, she doesn't let go of her own papers but picks up Wallace's bag with her left hand. From the bottom. She gives the bag what she hopes is an imperceptible shake, and the stacks of bills begin to slide out through the opening.

"You stupid—" Wallace starts.

Just as Zoe flings her elbow into his stomach.

It's not that she's strong, but she *has* caught him unawares.

He lets go of her right arm and doubles over, just a bit. In a moment he will straighten up, and Zoe knows he will be very, very angry. But in *this* moment she goes for the one self-defense move she knows: She brings her knee up into his groin.

Only . . .

He takes a step back.

So she misses.

And her advantage of surprise is over that quickly. He strides forward and strikes her with the back of his hand—a lot harder than she had managed to hit him.

Already badly positioned, she falls over.

She has heard people refer to *seeing stars* after a blow to the head, and had assumed this was simply a convention in cartoons. But now she sees stars, and they're exploding. Also, the room is spinning. But even with all of that going on she knows exactly where she is, and she expects to fall on Daniel.

Except she doesn't.

He has rolled out of the way.

Not—she suddenly realizes—to avoid her, but to get at his gun.

She realizes this because Wallace has already come to the same conclusion. Wallace has dropped to his knees, and now he pulls Zoe in front of him, using her as a shield, his arm once more around her neck. "So help me, I will kill her," he announces.

The stars from Zoe's vision clear, revealing Daniel on his knees also, his gun trained on Wallace behind her.

And she can feel Wallace's gun pressed against the side of her head.

Oh crap, Zoe thinks. This is like a replay of the original time, only now it's *her* in the middle. It doesn't help to think about how that first time ended.

Daniel asks, "What would killing her accomplish?"

"I don't want to," Wallace claims, which is a relief to hear. Only he undermines this by adding, "But I don't want to *get* killed."

Daniel says, "And that won't happen if you put the gun down."

"I don't want to get arrested either," Wallace says.

Daniel shakes his head. "Can't help you there," he admits. "But the penalty for attempted armed robbery is less than for murder." Very gently, almost pleading now, he says, "Put the gun down, Wallace."

Zoe feels the gun going tap-tap against her temple as Wallace's hand begins to shake.

"All I wanted," Wallace says, "was a fresh start."

"I understand," Daniel says.

The barrel of Wallace's gun digs firmly into Zoe's flesh. "Yeah?" Suddenly he's angry again. "Someone like you understands someone like me? Is that what you're saying?" He speaks very slowly and distinctly. "If I have to kill her, it will be your fault. It will be because *you* made me kill her. Are you so cocky you can live with that, Mr. Fancy-East-Ave.-Office P.I.? Knowing you made me kill her?"

"Killing her gains you nothing," Daniel tells him.

And Wallace finishes, "Except for the satisfaction of knowing you didn't want me to."

And that, Zoe thinks, *is that*. A deadlock. A dead end. A dead draw. *Stop thinking "dead,"* she tells herself. But, of course, she can't.

A voice behind Zoe announces, "Yeah, well, I don't want you to kill her either," and Zoe realizes it's bank guard Bobby. She guesses, by the way Wallace has stiffened, that Bobby has located the gun she saw go sliding under the furniture of the bank manager's office. She gathers that Bobby is holding *his* gun at *Wallace's* head. Wily P.I.

that he is, Daniel, who was facing that direction, had kept his face from showing anything during Bobby's approach, had kept his eyes from wavering off Wallace.

"Even if," Wallace says, "one or both of you get a shot off before I can, even if you put the bullet in my brain and I'm dead in an instant, in that instant my finger *will* tighten on the trigger, and she's dead."

Déjà vu, Zoe thinks. She knew what Wallace was going to say, before he said it, because she has heard him say much the same thing already.

And she has seen the result.

If she could get her mouth to work, she would warn Daniel to back up, because he's about to get her blood all over him. And she knows how hard it was for her to get *his* blood off *her*. It is only in this moment that she feels it is well and truly gone.

Daniel is still looking at Wallace, not at Zoe. Same as last time. He even has much the same scared and desperate look in his eyes as he did then, though it is not his life in danger. He says, "Nobody has to die."

Does his voice have a tremor? Or does it just sound that way to Zoe because she herself is shaking?

"You don't want to hurt her," Daniel says to Wallace. "And I'm willing to take her place. I'll walk out of here with you."

At which point Zoe's voice *does* work. "No," she tells Daniel, though every ounce of self-survival instinct is telling her to shut up. "He says he'll let me go once he's safely out of here. You said he wasn't a bad man. We have to trust him."

Zoe doesn't trust him. On a scale of one to ten, she fears her chance of survival is probably about one. But if Daniel takes her place, she suspects his chance will be lower.

Finally, finally, Daniel is looking at her. She's convinced he can read her mind. And, in turn, she can read his. They both know he's never going to agree to let Wallace take her out of here.

And apparently Wallace can read *their* minds, too. They are at an impasse. She feels him take a steadying breath. His arm tightens around her neck.

She remembers what it felt like to get shot, that run-into-by-a-freight-train feeling, but she also remembers that—at first—she didn't even know she'd been hit. Maybe she'll be lucky and this will be like that. Maybe she'll be dead before she knows it.

Zoe always wondered, when she read in history class about people getting their heads chopped off, how quick a death that was. Did Marie Antoinette, did Anne Boleyn, did Sir Thomas More die the instant the blade cut through their bodies—or did it take a second or two for their brains to stop sending signals? It would be kind of grim to think they might have gotten a dizzying, disorienting view of their place of execution as their severed heads bounced free from their bodies. To imagine that they had time to think: *Yikes! Is that my own headless body I just caught a glimpse of?*

Specifically, what Zoe is wondering—beyond how badly a bullet to the brain will hurt—is whether she'll be aware, as she falls, of the splatter of her blood on Daniel kneeling in front of her.

She closes her eyes, because she doesn't want to see.

Wallace can only kill you once, she reminds herself. She takes her stolen, wet, stupid, useless paperwork, and she smacks his face with it as hard as she can.

The sound of the gun going off is louder than she expected.

But the freight train is right on schedule.

164

CHAPTER 14

WELL, SHE HAD ASSUMED DYING WOULD BE FASTER.

And quieter.

Zoe opens her eyes a crack, determined to close them again quickly if there's the gunshot equivalent of any head-bouncing-off-the-executioner's-block view to be seen.

What she sees is Daniel, his blue eyes not six inches from her own. He's saying something, but she can't hear a thing over the ringing in her ears.

Ear. It's her right ear that seems to have become home to a vast and inexhaustible collection of clanging cymbals.

She goes to touch her right ear and finds Daniel's hand there already. She feels for her left ear, and her fingers brush Daniel's other hand—not covering that ear, but close by. Supporting her head? Maybe? She has to concentrate to get her bearings. She is sitting, not kneeling—which was her last recollection—and not lying down on the floor bleeding out. Or at least she doesn't think so. Surely she would know by now, even if she was a little slow about catching on that other time. But she doesn't want to embarrass herself by being the last to know, so she glances around for blood splatter.

None to be seen.

What she does see is one of the bank tellers unlocking the front door to let in the police. Customers and staff getting up off the floor.

And Wallace, face down on the ground practically within touching distance, his hands clasped behind his head, with Bobby's knee on his back, Bobby's gun pressed to the nape of his neck. Apparently Bobby is a better bank guard than Zoe has given him credit for. No one is dead.

No one is dead.

Not her. Not anyone.

"I didn't hurt her," Wallace is protesting. "And, even if she *was* hurt, that wouldn't've been my fault. My gun only went off accidentally when *you* ran into me."

"Oh," Zoe says to Bobby, not sure if she's whispering or shouting, "you overpowered him."

Bobby, looking a bit pasty and wobbly, manages a smile of sorts as he first shakes his head—well, it's more of a twitch—then nods toward Daniel to indicate *he* was the one who did the running-into. But before Zoe can turn to thank Daniel, Bobby indicates for her to look up to the ceiling.

There's a hole, with plaster dust still wafting down like a late-season sprinkling of snow—just like Rochester in March. Or April. Sometimes May . . .

She forces herself to focus. She wasn't knocked over by the force of the bullet hitting her, but by Daniel tackling Wallace, forcing his gun arm up so that he fired into the ceiling.

"Thank you," she says to, or shouts at, Daniel.

He takes his hand away from her ear, which makes the noise in her head get louder.

"Ringing?" he asks sympathetically.

She can hear him through her left ear, over the racket in her right. She nods because she doesn't want to be obnoxiously loud, like those hard-of-hearing people who refuse to admit they *are* hard of hearing. She presses her own hand against her ear, even though she liked it better when Daniel was doing it.

Charlotte has come up behind Daniel and is looking at Zoe appraisingly. "Tinnitus," she proclaims.

Daniel nods. "Should go away over the next few hours."

Well, that's a relief to know.

Charlotte is nodding, too. Until she helpfully adds, "Unless there's permanent hearing loss. That happened to my brother-in-law when he set off illegal fireworks two summers ago. But you should know, one way or the other, within twenty-four hours."

Daniel scowls at Charlotte, but she doesn't notice because she's leaning in close to Zoe. "Thank you," she tells Zoe. "You were very brave."

"Very, very brave," Daniel amends.

"No." Zoe shakes her head, because she *knows* how terrified she was.

But Charlotte nods emphatically. She says, "I was not. I was, in fact, a disappointment to myself. I will hold you up as a model."

Is she serious? It's hard to keep a grudge against someone who says something like that seriously.

Paramedics have come in after the police, and a pair of them kneel beside and in front of Zoe, displacing Charlotte, which is no great loss, but also Daniel. "Hey," one of them says to her, in that jovial tone medical professionals use when they don't want you to worry, "how are you doing?"

"Tinnitus," Zoe explains, probably too softly or too loudly.

The paramedic makes a dismissive gesture. "Not to worry. That'll only last a few hours."

Daniel winks at her, then goes off to answer questions for the police.

She assumes he'll have the sense not to talk about playback, because she certainly has no intention of bringing it up.

The paramedics look her over just short of forever. They inform her that she has a powder burn on her right temple, from the gun going off so close. It didn't hurt until she knew about it, but now it's hot and sore. They tell her that this, too, should go away sooner rather than later.

Partway through their examination, she glances to where she last saw Daniel, wondering how he's doing, but apparently the police have finished questioning him. He's no longer there. She looks around. The bank is not that big: Daniel is gone. *Oh*, she thinks. Not that she had any right to expect him to hang around and wait for her. She has no right to feel disappointed. What did she expect? She's known him a lot longer than he's known her.

The paramedics talk and talk at her, wanting to bring her to the hospital for observation, but she finally convinces them that she feels fine.

Then it's her turn with the police. *They* talk and talk at her, wanting more details, but she finally convinces *them* that at the moment she can't think straight because she has a splitting headache due to the tinnitus. She doesn't mention that the noise level inside her head is beginning to move down the scale from full cacophony to simple clamor. She gives them her parents' old Thurston Road address rather than saying she lives in a group home on Newell, and promises she will report to the downtown precinct office tomorrow to give her statement. She's trying to leave them with the impression that she's here with one of the other customers, a responsible adult, and she is just wondering how she is going to get out of the bank without anyone noticing she is in fact alone, when she sees that Daniel has returned.

He nods to the two police officers who have been talking to her, then asks, "Ready to go home, Zoe?" as though he's the responsible adult in charge of her.

Outside, the rain has finally stopped, though the sidewalk has puddles the size of small ponds. There are crowds of onlookers, including reporters from the local news. But Daniel has timed their exit to coincide with that of the bank manager, who is giving an official statement, and they make it past the police tape without anyone stopping them. Daniel has hold of her arm.

"I'm going   " —Zoe nods across the street —"that way." It's sort of the way back to the group home. Not the most direct route. But *a* way. She knows she has to make peace with Mrs. Davies eventually.

"I'll drive you home," Daniel says. "We need to talk. Get our stories aligned before we go to the police tomorrow. My car is parked behind the building where we met."

"Oh," Zoe says, letting him guide her in the direction he wants to go. She suspects he won't be fooled with the Thurston Road address, with her asking to be dropped off by the curb. Suspects it won't be enough for her to wave good-bye from in front of the house, but that he intends to see her safely inside. "I live in a group home," she admits. "That is, unless Mrs. Davies has had me kicked out."

Daniel raises his eyebrows.

"Those papers . . ." She stops walking. Where *are* her papers?

She hasn't thought about them since using them to smack Wallace. On other playbacks, she's left them behind, but she's never before forgotten them. She supposes this is a sign.

Of something.

She resumes walking. "Those papers I had? I thought . . . I don't know . . . that if I took them before anybody could upload them onto the computer, if I destroyed them, then it would be like that part of my life hadn't happened. Like erasing one story and starting another. Anyway, I may have burned some bridges. I called my housemother some pretty ugly names when she caught me taking them."

Daniel is looking a bit perplexed. "But wouldn't the doctors and social workers who made the evaluations have their own copies in any case?"

Of course they would. Zoe feels about seven years old. That pre–Mrs. Davies housemother was right: *Too impulsive. Too impatient. Doesn't think of consequences.* "Where were you to give advice when I needed it?"

Daniel counters, "How likely would you have been to take advice if I had been there to give it?"

Zoe shrugs.

"I'm guessing," Daniel continues, "that the kind of person who becomes a housemother has probably heard—and forgiven—a lot of name-calling. Anyway, I fully intend to tell her how heroically you acted today."

"Yeah, right," Zoe scoffs.

Daniel repeats what he said in the bank: "You were very, very brave."

170

"I was not."

"You were."

"Was not."

"Were."

Now they're both sounding about seven.

He isn't going to concede, so she says, "I'm not going to try to explain playing back time."

"I should hope not," Daniel says. "I told the police you came to me after you saw Wallace in his car and spotted his gun. And I'll tell your housemother the same thing."

They're almost at the Fitzhugh House. She doesn't want to talk about what they've just been through, about dying and almost dying and finally—finally—nobody dying. Later, yes—but now is too soon. To cover maybe five more seconds before they reach the door, Zoe uses conversation filler. She says, "So, you have a brother. Is he younger or older than you?"

Daniel stops walking. "How could you know about the trust fund, but not about my brother?"

Maybe it's the tinnitus. Or the powder burn, which is beginning to throb. Zoe admits, "I'm . . . not seeing the connection."

He's obviously trying to read her face. He must come to the conclusion that she's confused, not playing games, because he explains, "It's a special needs trust fund, to take care of my brother in case he outlives our parents and me."

"*Special needs?*" Zoe echoes. "As in . . . ?"

"He has schizophrenia."

That explains why Daniel was not freaked out by her history.

He adds, "Pete has a janitorial job at the bank. That's how the people there know him."

Zoe is coming to distrust a lot of the conclusions she's made over the day. People can be more complicated than she has been giving them credit for. "I thought you were rich," she says.

"Ah," he says. "Me and my Mercedes Benz."

"You have a Mercedes?" she asks.

"I have a Saturn station wagon."

"They stopped making Saturns *years* ago," she protests, knowing this only because her family had a Saturn from the last year the company was in business.

"Even so . . . ," he says.

When she eventually realizes he isn't going to say anything else, she says, "But you have expensive clothing. And, apparently, an impressive office in an old-monied section of town."

"*One* expensive jacket," he corrects her. "A *small* office. Clients aren't going to trust an investigator who looks like the kind of guy who has to borrow money from his parents."

"*Have* you had to borrow money from your parents?"

"Not yet," Daniel says. "Hence the Saturn. Until the college loans are paid off."

"Not Harvard?" Zoe says, remembering how she almost lost credibility by taking Wallace at his word. "Or Yale? Princeton?"

"State University of New York at Brockport, with just enough scholarship to make it almost seem doable."

"Wow," she says. "Times are tough for young P.I.'s."

"Oh," he says, "I'm hoping times will get better. If you can continue to keep me from getting killed."

"Hmmm," she says. Very aware of his exact wording. Very aware that he did not say simply, *If I can keep from getting killed.* She turns it back onto him. "It seems as though *you* turned out to be pretty good at keeping *me* from getting killed, too."

"But I only had to do it once," he points out. "Here,"—he pulls a cell phone from his pocket—"things are not so tough that I can't afford a small token of appreciation for you." She's seen his phone often enough to know this isn't it. "I got it at the wireless kiosk behind the bank while the paramedics were still checking you over," he explains when she looks at him blankly.

"What is it?" she asks suspiciously.

Very slowly he enunciates, "It's. A. Cell. Phone."

"For me?" Zoe asks. The noise in her ear is still diminishing, but her brain seems to have liquefied. "You bought that for *me*?"

"No, for your housemother," Daniel says in exasperation.

Zoe shakes her head.

Daniel continues nonetheless. "There's a digital clock. So you'll always know what time it is. Plus, you can call for help. If you need it. So you don't always have to do *everything* all by yourself."

"I don't *always* have to do *everything* all by myself," Zoe protests, feeling that his words make her sound pigheaded and inflexible. Which . . .

All right, all right, *maybe*. Sometimes. A little bit. But only because she has to be.

Except then she thinks back to her mother with the gun at the Family Counseling Center. Everything does *not* always have to come down to her. Even without her, everyone survived that time, too. More or less. Not her family as a whole, of course. Her father sued for divorce from his hospital bed. Her mother signed the papers while in her jail cell. Zoe ended up in a group home. The counselor closed his practice and moved to Florida with his receptionist. Life moved on, and yet Zoe cannot honestly say whether things are better or worse for what happened back then.

Zoe informs Daniel, "It's not like I *choose* to be a loner."

He says, "Uh-huh. Can you say that a second time with a straight face?"

It doesn't help that he looks ready to laugh at her. She counters by saying, "Blitzen."

Daniel clearly has no idea how to take that. "*Blitzen*," he repeats.

"*Not*," she tells him, knowing it's no clarification for him, "William Henry Harrison."

"OK," Daniel says, slow and uncertain. They have not discussed reindeer this past twenty-three minutes. They have never discussed U.S. presidents.

Zoe relents and explains, "I just acknowledged you're right."

Daniel nods, still not looking entirely convinced. But then, still with no way of understanding, he buys into it. He goes back to explaining about the phone. "It's pay-as-you-go. Prepaid for one year or a thousand minutes. If you need more minutes, you're on your own, so easy with the texting. I've already programmed my number into it, so if you need me—for anything—you can reach me."

"I appreciate it," Zoe says. "Truly I do." She uses the word *truly* intentionally—despite the fact that even if he could remember their previous playbacks, still, he wouldn't realize this is one of *his* words, not hers. And, in any case, now that she *has* used the word, she regrets it because it sounds like the end of a letter. And ends are sad and scary because you can never be sure what's coming next. She won't let herself think about that, so she, too, goes back to the phone. "But we aren't allowed—"

Daniel cuts her off. "I will have a good long talk with your housemother, explaining it's an issue of safety." He considers. "And if I can't convince her . . ."

It's Zoe's turn to interrupt. "Then I can hide it."

Daniel shakes his head, but it's not to disagree with her. He muses, "Here I am, contributing to the delinquency of a minor . . ."

Zoe's heart is doing odd flip-flops.

She's almost sixteen.

He's almost twenty-five.

It is—at this point in their lives—an insurmountable difference.

But it won't always be.

He's just being nice, she tells herself. *Older-brotherly nice.* Not that she's thinking of him in a brotherly way. But if she pushes now, if she's impatient and impulsive and doesn't think ahead to the future, she's just going to end up embarrassing herself and—more importantly—cutting off possibilities for that future. She's done that often enough before. She will not do it now.

You were very, very brave, Daniel told her. Twice now. And Charlotte said it, too.

There's more to being brave than risking your life.

Sometimes, you need to risk everything.

There will be a lot of twenty-three-minute intervals between now and when she's old enough—even going through them only once. A lot of things can change in that amount of time.

But she forces herself to say no more than, "I promise I won't abuse your friendship."

He responds to the seriousness in her tone with a slow,

thoughtful "OK" that simultaneously shakes and strengthens her resolve. Then he smiles and asks, "Come in with me? While I trade Milo back for my jacket?"

"Sure," Zoe tells him. "Even though you're only asking me because you think you need a chaperone when you're with him."

He laughs as they start up the front stairs.

Oh, she likes that laugh every bit as much as she likes the "OK."

She's used to playing back time to try to fix things gone wrong. This once, she almost wishes she could play back just one minute, this last minute, simply to savor it. But she can't. So she'll play it back only in her mind, the way everyone else does, because—anyway—she wouldn't dare risk changing a second of it.

As the start for a new story, Zoe thinks it's just about perfect.